D0698985

Saddle a Whirlwind

Saddle a Whirlwind

Eugene C. Vories

Walker and Company
New York

First published in the United States of America in 1990
by Walker Publishing Company, Inc.

Published simultaneously in Canada by Thomas Allen & Son
Canada, Limited, Markham, Ontario

Library of Congress Cataloging-in-Publication Data

Vories, Eugene C.
Saddle a whirlwind / Eugene C. Vories.
ISBN 0-8027-4106-1
I. Title
PS3572.056S24   1990
813′.54—dc20   90-35569
CIP

Printed in the United States of America

2   4   6   8   10   9   7   5   3   1

CHAPTER 1

THIS was the first time Becky Major had seen her brother Vance in over three weeks. He had come to see her in town and she was determined to find out about the ranch. She knew Vance would try to put up a good front to keep her from worrying. He had always been that way, but even more so now because she had held out the longest against the family borrowing money from Carl Farr to buy livestock. She couldn't blame him for putting a good picture on things as he would sure not want her to be able to say, "I told you so."

Their father had heavily mortgaged the ranch, and the bank had insisted the family sell all the cattle to pay off the notes when the old man died. Without cattle the ranch was worthless. With the oldest son Harvey's help and connection, Carl Farr had seemed glad to loan them money to restock. Farr was Harvey's father-in-law, a successful rancher from a wealthy eastern family, not a real westerner. Vance had contracted for cattle but they would not be delivered for another month or two. Naturally they had to put up the deeded land, as well as the cattle they were buying, to secure the loan from Farr. The big rancher had seemed cordial and agreeable at the time of the loan, and Becky could only hope they could make enough that year to meet the first payment.

"Grass looks good," Vance was saying in his deep voice and abrupt manner of speech. "It sure helped to be resting it this spring."

He and their longtime ranch hand Monte sat at the kitchen table. Vance was young, in the prime of his manhood; the other was old, stiff, and white haired. They watched as Becky bent her trim figure to take two pumpkin pies from the oven

1

of the big range. She slid one pie on a plump pot holder placed on the oilcloth table cover. The other was placed on the enameled top of the kitchen cabinet.

"You know what I'm concerned about," she said as she slid the pot holder with the pie between the two men. "I don't trust Carl Farr, no matter how close Harvey is to him. Has he made any move to bring stock in on our grass?"

"Not a sign of it," Vance assured her, his attention now intently on the pie. "I don't think Farr is the one who'll move in on us. We've got several neighbors closer than him and some of them need grass a lot more than Farr does. Sid and Russ have eaten their places into the ground the last few years. I know they have always wanted a part of our grass. I'll admit I'm worried, Sis, but so far no real trouble. We've pushed a few cows off but not many more than usual."

"Have you been able to hire any riders?" she asked.

"No. Sure haven't," Vance said abruptly. "Funny, too. Last year there was always someone wanting a job. This year you can't find a man out of work."

"Even Joe Vigil is riding steady for Payne," old Monte added, his faded blue eyes admiring the pie before him. "First full-time job he's held in years."

Vance's dark brown eyes suddenly sparkled and his sunburned lips parted in one of his rare sly smiles. "Let Monte cut the pie," he said abruptly but softly, not looking at her.

"Oh, sure, let Monte cut it!" Becky exclaimed in pretended anger. "I'm on to you fellows. Monte only knows how to cut a pie in quarters."

"Only way," the old man grunted. Monte's speech was always punctuated with a grunt. "Sure looks good. Smells good, too. Since Vance asked, I'll do the honors."

The white-haired old cowman quickly reached behind the woman to get a knife from the cupboard drawer. With a flourish, he cut the pie into four equal pieces. He slid a piece onto each of the plates she put before them. A moment later he tossed Vance a fork and the two men went at the pie with relish. Becky smiled and poured coffee for them both.

"You going to have some pie, Becky?" the old man asked between bites.

"No, I'll wait until after supper."

"I hope there's some left, then." Monte grunted and returned his attention to his plate.

The two ate in silence for a few minutes. Becky watched in amusement. She knew them both so well, and she could not help feeling they were not telling her everything about the neighbors and their grass.

"Just when is school out?" Vance asked as his piece of pie was almost gone.

She had taken care of Vance's two children ever since his wife had died. Now, the three of them lived in town at the big old house on Third Street. Vance usually came in every few weeks during the winter months to be with his children for a day or two. During the summer, Becky and the children spent most of their time at the ranch with him. Vance was the only member of the Major family living at the ranch. The other sisters were married and lived in town, as did the older brother. Harvey Major was sheriff in Sundown.

"I think school gets out May fifteenth this year. That's still almost two months."

"You and the children be out the sixteenth?"

"I suppose so, Vance. Maybe I can take them out a few days early. They have done well this year. I'll speak to Miss Marshall about it. She understands how much you want them with you."

"Well, we could sure use your help, too," Vance said, his bronze face not covering the tension he was under. "There is so much country we need to keep an eye on, the four of us can't get to all of it often enough. Juan needs to start the three-year-olds, so that means one less rider. You and the kids could sure help us cover more country."

"Besides, you want the children home," Becky added

knowingly. She knew so well the two children were the most important thing in his lonely life. "I'll come as soon as I can. Helen talked like she wouldn't mind coming out, too, this summer. She could help cook and do the laundry. That would let me ride more. She thinks Frank and the boys should not only get along without her but also would probably enjoy it."

"That would be great," Monte said, eyeing the half pie still in the pie pan. "But, you could keep on makin' pies. Helen is a good cook but not quite as good as you are on pie."

"No flattery, please, Monte . . . go ahead, help yourself," she said, smiling. She shoved the pan toward the old man. "At your age, what you eat won't hurt you."

"Never has, yet," the old man replied, helping himself to another piece of pie before pushing the pan toward Vance. "A few meals I missed hurt me more than anything I ever ate. . . . Sure be good to have you back at the ranch, Becky. We do need riders, real riders."

Becky's brown eyes, as dark as her brother's, went to the old man's face. Was Monte trying to tell her something Vance was holding back? Monte had taught her to ride and work cattle. Had taught her much about the ranch and cattle business, but he had never acted as though he believed any woman could really help with the ranch work. Women were nice to have around the house, to cook and wash clothes, but never before had he indicated she could be of help as a rider. She studied the old face—it might tell her more than her brother's words ever would. The man tugged at the drooping white mustache, as he often did when trying to hide the expression on his face. She read the concern he was trying not to show in his eyes. She knew instinctively that there was trouble at the ranch, as she had feared there might be.

Vance must really be afraid the neighbors would begin pushing in on their grass, she thought. Farr was perhaps only waiting for the grass to get a little higher, as it would later in the spring. Well, she had tried to get the family to look elsewhere for money.

They all knew she had never liked the idea of them borrowing money from Carl Farr. She knew all too well the risk they had taken. If they lost their grass for the cattle they had coming and could not pay the big man's note, Farr would wind up owning the ranch her family had called theirs for as long as she could remember.

She knew, too, an empty pasture, especially if it was public range, was always a tremendous temptation to any neighboring rancher. All ranchers always had their eye on the range bordering theirs. Several of their neighbors had long wanted the open range they used. It was human nature to want to grow bigger. Besides, several of the smaller ranches around them had abused their places until they no longer would support the number of cattle they needed to make a living. Yes, the little neighbors would try to push in on them but it was Carl Farr that worried her the most. They could handle the small ranchers. But Farr was a big operator and had a crew of cowboys who would probably enjoy a range war. A worried frown crossed her pretty face. Damn bankers and loan people, anyway.

The band of horses ran along the side of the deep arroyo, a big roan mare in the lead. The mare's colt strained his long, gangly legs to keep up with his mother. The old mare was wise in the ways of a wild animal. Men had corralled her before and she was determined to avoid entrapment again. The band of mares, colts, and older geldings would follow any lead she made. As usual, the stud stayed at the rear of the band encouraging the stragglers, with teeth bared and ears laid back.

A branch arroyo broke off toward the main creek ahead of them and the mare swerved sharply, going down the loose, sandy soil of the bank at breakneck speed. Her colt whinnied in fright and excitement, his mouth open sucking in his breath. Without hesitation, he followed his mother. He had to jump off a three-foot bank at the floor of the almost dry creek bed, his long legs thrashing about wildly. He almost fell but regained his balance.

The riders cursed the old mare. They had been pushing the horses, trying to keep them on this side of the creek. A running horse usually avoided sudden changes of direction but not that old mare.

Vance Major jabbed spurs against his horse's sides and urged it ahead at top speed. He could not cross the creek until he got to the place the horses had gone over the bank. He had to cross and turn the herd if they were going to corral them. He forced his horse to turn down the slope the others had taken. As his horse raced down the bank, dust boiled up around the cut from the herd's passing. He could not see the ground ahead, as the dust blinded him. It must have blinded his horse as well, for suddenly a sickening sensation went through his stomach as the horse collapsed under him. The horse had not seen the last drop-off. Vance desperately tried to grab the saddle horn to catch his balance and furiously jerked on the reins to help his horse regain its footing. He felt the horse roll underneath him and a terrible pain grated through his right foot and lower leg, then all went black.

He became conscious to find the crushing weight of the horse pushing him deeper into the wet, sandy soil as the animal struggled to right itself. Again, he felt excruciating pain and he sank back into unconsciousness.

Water splashed over his face and he opened his eyes. Above him, Monte's worried old face was peering down at him. The old man's white hair and drooping mustache were plain to him.

"That's it, Vance . . . come out of it, boy," Monte encouraged. The old cowman splashed more water from his hat brim onto Vance's face and neck.

"Don't drown me, Monte!" Vance exclaimed. "I had a bath last Saturday."

"You sure wouldn't know it now. We drug your horse off you . . . had to shoot him. He had a broke leg."

"I think I do, too," Vance muttered as the pain hit him again. "My right foot sure hurts like hell."

Juan Martinez was kneeling at Vance's feet. He gently picked up the right boot and Vance called out in pain.

"God, don't do that! I could feel the bones grating."

"We'll have to get that boot off," Monte said. "Is it your leg or your ankle?"

"Both, I think."

"Damn the luck," the old cowboy swore. "Things was goin' so good, too."

"Can you stand for me to pull your boot off?" Juan asked.

"I don't think so, but try it."

The instant Juan put the slightest pressure on the foot, the injured man's shouts stopped him. Tears rolled from Vance's deep brown eyes.

"Cut it off," he instructed through gritted teeth. "Don't look like I'll wear a boot again for a while, anyway. Damn the luck. This sure puts us in one hell of a spot. I can't waste time with a broken leg."

Juan unbuckled Vance's spur and his sharp knife sliced through the upper boot. When he had to put pressure on the instep, Vance screamed and lapsed back into unconsciousness. Old Monte turned to the big bearded man who was holding their horses on the arroyo bank above them.

"Bud, you ride to the ranch as fast as you can. You'll have to run the horses in and harness the team. Hook up the wagon and put a mattress and some blankets in it. Bedsprings, too, would help."

"All right." Big Bud Jarvis moved in slow, deliberate motions without the slightest sign of excitement.

"I'll go with him," Juan said, his job with the knife finished. "It'll be faster with two of us."

"All right, Juan. Bring my horse over here where I can hold him," Monte agreed readily, knowing Juan would do it with all speed. Bud never hurried. "Bring something we can use for a stretcher to carry him up out of here. Get the wagon as close as you can."

Bud led Monte's horse close and the old man's gnarled hand reached out to grasp the bridle reins of the big bay. He poured the rest of the water from his hat over Vance's face as the other two swung into their saddles and spurred hard down the creek bed.

Vance drifted in and out of consciousness. Monte laid the man's head in his lap and held Vance's hat where it would shield the man's face from the sun.

"This is a bad deal, Monte," the short cowboy said when he came to again. "Sure hope Doc can set this so I can get back here before those cows get here."

"I'm sure he can," Monte lied and hoped the man believed him. "Doc's pretty good. He fixed Harvey's leg just fine."

"That's sure right."

"I sent the boys for the wagon. It'll be a hell of a ride but we've got to get you to town."

"I'll make it," Vance said, his usual determination showing in his eyes, along with the pain he felt.

It was almost two hours before the men got there with the wagon. Juan came running down the bank, carrying an old door he brought to use as a stretcher. He and Monte laid this beside Vance.

"Let's put his upper body on it first," Monte said. "Then we'll ease his legs over. Where the hell is Bud?"

"Tying the team, I guess."

"Come on, Bud!" Monte yelled. "We need some help—now!"

The big man trotted down the bank, his lack of concern showing plainly beneath his beard. Monte lifted Vance to an almost sitting position and Juan slid the door behind him. Monte eased Vance down on the door as gently as he could.

"Bud, get on the other side across from Juan and see if you can lift his butt up enough for me to slide this door under his hips."

Bud kneeled slowly across from the slender Mexican. The two lifted as gently as they could and Monte shoved the door.

"Bud, you'll have to roll him your way some, I can't push the door under him with Juan sitting there."

Bud reached over and began rolling Vance slowly toward him. Juan jumped back and swung the door under the man's hips.

"That's it, now roll him back on the door."

Vance cried out in pain as they moved him. Monte and Juan gently lifted the pants leg of the injured foot and eased the leg onto the door. Again Vance cried out. Monte swung his other leg onto the door.

"He's too far down," Monte said. "See if the two of you can ease him up that way a little and I'll try to lift his foot."

Sweat poured off Vance's face and rolled around his neck. He wiped it with his hand and licked his lips as Monte made sure they had him in the right position.

Monte and Juan each took a corner of the door at Vance's feet and Bud got the middle of the door at his head. Slowly they stood up and started up the bank, Juan and Monte in the lead. They had to move very slowly and cautiously to find footing. Soft dirt slid under them at each step.

"Hold your end a little higher if you can, Bud," Monte said, trying his utmost to keep the door level and maintain steady footing.

"I can hold it as high as you want," Bud said through his beard. "This ain't heavy to me."

As though to prove his strength, the big man lifted the door shoulder high.

"Not so high! Not so high, damn it!" Monte snapped. "Just hold him level."

The two men in front were exhausted by the time they

reached the wagon but Bud had not seemed to exert himself. The big man was plainly proud of his superior strength.

"Bud, put your end on the end gate a minute," Monte told the big man as his own chest heaved. "How the hell are we gonna transfer him to the mattress?"

"Let's put the door up along one side of the wagon bed and see if we can slide him off onto the mattress," Juan said. He let Monte hold their end of the door alone while he jumped lithely into the wagon bed.

It took time, as each move was misery for Vance. The sun was now dipping toward the west as they made the man as comfortable as they could on the mattress and covered him well with blankets. The evening chill of the early spring afternoon was already descending upon them. Juan ran down the bank and got Monte's horse to lead the big bay back and tie it to the end gate of the wagon. Bud removed Vance's saddle and bridle from the dead horse and threw them in beside the injured man.

"You drive, Juan," Monte instructed. "I'll ride back here with Vance. Don't let them horses out of a slow walk. Every move is going to hurt him."

The Mexican climbed onto the seat and unfastened the lines from the brake handle. Bud climbed up beside him and Juan eased the horses ahead. They had gone only a few feet when Monte hollered for them to stop.

"God, I never knowed this ground was that rough!" the old cowman exclaimed. "It's jarring him to pieces. Let me have those lines and you two get out and walk with the horses. Try to ease the wagon over each clump of grass."

"It will help some when we get to the road," Juan said as he jumped down.

Bud slowly and deliberately climbed over the wheel to the ground. When each man was at the head of one of the team, Monte slackened the lines and they moved ahead slowly.

In spite of their utmost efforts, Vance cried out in pain at each bump. Even to Monte, the ground seemed to have only mountains and valleys. Normally, he would have driven the team over this kind of ground at a high trot, even a lope. It took hours for them to reach the road. Night had long since come and their only light was from a big full moon.

Now it was smoother. When they finally reached the road Monte stopped to let the others get back on the seat, and he climbed back over the seat to squat beside Vance. Juan spoke to the team and let them walk slowly ahead. The horses wanted to go to their accustomed trot and each time one tried to break his gait, Juan spoke in firm tones and gave a quick jerk on the line.

"Don't let them out of a slow walk," Monte instructed again.

"I'm thirsty as hell, Monte," the injured man said, speaking for the first time in hours. "Have you got anything to drink?"

"Sorry, Vance, I never thought to bring any water."

"I'd like something a lot stronger than water," Vance said between parched lips. "Bud got any whiskey?"

"You got any whiskey on you, Bud?" Monte stretched his neck over the seat to ask.

"Hell, no! You know what you told me."

"Wish now I hadn't been quite so firm," the white-haired old cowman grunted as he squatted back down. "Don't know if you should have whiskey or not, Vance, but I could sure use some."

The hours dragged on as they crept at a snail's pace along the road. The injured man either slept or passed out from pain most of the time, Monte was not sure which. The old man rolled a smoke. When he saw Vance's eyes were open in the light of his match, he offered the man the cigarette.

"No, thanks, Monte. I'm so dry now it would only make it worse."

Monte drew in a lungful of smoke, the end of his cigarette glowing angrily in the darkness.

"You shouldn't smoke in bed, Monte," Juan said over his shoulder, having caught a whiff of the tobacco smoke. He remembered all too well the sermon the old rider had given him on this subject.

"Well, I sure as hell ain't gonna fall asleep tonight," the old man snapped back.

It was nearly daybreak when they drew the wagon to a halt at Doc Jacobs's house.

"Go get the doc, Bud," Monte instructed. "It may take me a week to get my legs operatin' again."

"It's colder than I thought it would be," Juan said and turned to flash his smile at the old man as he rubbed his arms briskly. "How's Vance?"

"Been asleep or out for an hour," Monte grunted. "Sure glad we brought blankets for him."

Eventually the doctor came, carrying a kerosene lantern and his black bag. He was dressed in a nightshirt, heavy coat, and slippers.

"Take him right on up to my office," he instructed without looking at the injured man. "I can't do anything until I get him there anyway."

The wagon creaked again as the horses pulled against their collars. The doctor's office and two-bed hospital were only a few houses down the street. By the time Juan swung the team and backed the wagon as close to the door as he could, the doctor had the door opened and a lamp lit.

"Have to get a stretcher," Doc Jacobs instructed. "We can't get that mattress through the door."

Juan climbed up beside Monte and the two managed to roll Vance over, place the stretcher behind him, and roll him back onto it, following the doctor's instructions at each step. Bud and the doctor then carried the man inside to the operating table.

"One of you men go get my nurse Mrs. Miller," Doc said as he cut Vance's pants leg up the seam to expose a now terribly swollen foot and ankle.

"Where does she live?" Monte asked.

"I know," Juan said. "I'll go get her."

Monte turned to the big puncher. "Bud, you go get the girls and Harvey. They'll have to know about this."

By now, the doctor was examining the ankle. Vance tried to sit up and screamed out in pain. The doctor went to a cabinet and selected a bottle. He poured a spoonful of liquid and pushed it between Vance's lips.

"Maybe that will help some," he said. "As soon as Mrs. Miller is here, we'll put you under while I look at that foot."

"Can you tell anything, Doc?" Monte asked.

"I'm afraid the ankle bones are crushed," Doc said and watched Vance's face. When the man closed his eyes, the doctor gave Monte a sharp glance and shook his head.

"Can you save it, Doc?" Vance asked. His eyes were still closed but he seemed to have sensed the doctor's look.

"I don't know," the doctor said honestly. "I'll have to go in and see how badly the bones are broken."

"Well, you set them somehow," Vance said, his voice deep and steady. "I don't want to be a one-legged cowboy."

"Oh, it won't come to that," Monte assured him.

"It hadn't better. If I wake up and find that foot ain't attached to my leg, I'm going to shoot both of you!" Vance promised sternly. "Monte, don't you let him take that foot off . . . no matter what!"

Monte looked down at the younger man. He had helped raise Vance from a boy. He knew the man well. His own faded blue eyes held a helpless look. How was he supposed to know when a thing like that had to be done?

"You hear me, Monte?" Vance asked, his eyes wide, fighting the effects of the drug the doctor had given him.

"I hear you, Vance. It won't come to that."

"Don't you leave me alone with this old butcher . . . not for a minute! If he starts to saw on that leg, you shoot him dead. I'd rather take a chance on them bones healin' by themselves than to have that foot cut off. You hear me, Monte?"

"I hear you, Vance."

Mrs. Miller bustled into the room, shedding her coat as

she entered. It was now daylight and the doctor blew out some of the lamps. Mrs. Miller went immediately to her work, washing her hands thoroughly and lighting the kerosene burner under the doctor's instrument pan. The doctor laid his tools on a tray. Mrs. Miller applied ether to cotton and placed it over Vance's nose.

"He's asleep now," she said a few minutes later. "You had better wait outside in the front room with the others," she told Monte as they heard the noise of the Major family arriving in the outer office.

"I ain't goin' nowhere," Monte stated firmly. "I'm staying right here. I promised that boy you would save his foot."

"I hope I can, Monte," the doctor said fervently. "I hope I can."

Monte was almost sick at his stomach as the doctor's scalpel sliced between the muscles of Vance's ankle. At last the bones were exposed.

"It's completely crushed, Monte, just as I was afraid," Doc muttered. "There's no way I can put those bones back together."

"You'd better try," Monte said softly.

"There's no way they'll heal so he can ever walk on it again. I'll have to take that foot off."

In the silence that followed Doc's statement came the sound of Monte cocking the Colt .45 in his gnarled old hand. In the stillness it sounded as loud as a cannon.

"Monte, you wouldn't! Vance will understand! He'll have to!"

"I promised," Monte replied softly. "You just put it together as best you can or, by God, I will shoot you! Save Vance the trouble."

"Monte, there is no way!"

"I suggest you think of something, invent something, or say your prayers." The white mustache bristled under Monte's nose and the aged blue eyes stared back at the wide ones of the doctor and his nurse.

Did the old man mean it? Doc wondered. It was impossible! Surely Monte would never pull the trigger!

"Now, Monte," Mrs. Miller said in a soothing tone and started around the table.

"You just stay over there and help Doc, Mrs. Miller. Vance didn't mention what to do with you, but you just help the doctor or I'll think of something."

"You wouldn't!"

"Mrs. Miller, I am a tired old cowboy, ain't slept a wink in over twenty-four hours. My thinkin' ain't too swift at best, so don't push your luck. I've worked for the Majors since Vance was a boy and I have never yet gone against a Major order. There is no way I'll go against what Vance told me."

"Silver wire!" Doc Jacobs suddenly exclaimed softly. "I read something recently where some doctor wired a man's bones and joints together with silver wire. I've never done it or seen it done, but he claimed it worked."

"Well, get some."

"I don't know where."

"If I get you some silver wire, will you try?" Monte asked.

"Do I have a choice?"

"No, but if I had your promise, I'd put this gun up and go find some wire."

"I promise to try, Monte. I have no hopes it will work but I will try."

Monte let the hammer down and shoved the pistol into his holster. He hurried as fast as his stiff, bowed legs would let him to the door of the outer office. He opened it slowly and stuck his head out. The three Major sisters looked up excitedly and their tall, dark brother pushed away from the wall to come toward him.

"Harvey," Monte said, "you and Juan go find Pancho Vigil. He's a silversmith and he should have some silver wire. Doc needs it. Get it quick as you can."

"How much?" Harvey Major asked, his dark eyes snapping.

"I don't know. Several feet. Hell, get all he has, we'll give him back what we don't use."

The tall man turned quickly as Juan jumped to open the outer door. It slammed behind them and Monte heard the sounds of their running feet fade away.

"Is Vance all right?" Becky asked, concern plain in her dark brown eyes. "Will he be all right?"

"I hope so, Becky. Doc's doing everything he can."

Monte went back into the operating room, where Doc and Mrs. Miller worked to expose as much of the broken bones as they could. Doc fitted some of the pieces of the joint together.

"How will I twist the wire tight?" Doc muttered to himself.

"I twist wire with wire pliers," Monte told him bluntly. "Hell, that thing there on your tray should do. Silver wire will be soft as anything."

"Monte, wash your hands thoroughly," Doc snapped.

"What?"

"Wash your hands thoroughly. Mrs. Miller will show you how," Doc repeated. "You'll have to twist the wire for me when I get the bones in place."

"I'm no doctor."

"You are now, you stubborn old coot. You insisted I do this, now you'll have to help. Hell, you operated on livestock all your life. This isn't much different."

Monte tossed his hat to the floor and hurried to the wash basin.

"Scrub your nails good," Doc muttered. "This may not work, probably won't, but Vance will have to be as mad at you as he is at me. I'm sure gonna tell him it's your fault if it don't work."

Minutes later, Harvey Major and Juan brought a roll of silver wire. Mrs. Miller uncoiled it, cut some off, and placed it in the boiling water of Doc's sterilizer. When it had had time to cook good, Doc took a piece out with his forceps. The wire was too hot to touch and they waited impatiently for it to cool. Then the doctor worked with the pieces of bone, coiling the wire around the pieces. It took both his and Mrs. Miller's fingers to hold everything in place.

"Put a couple of drops of ether on the cotton on Vance's nose," Doc told Monte. "We don't want him waking up now." Monte did as he was told.

"Now, Monte, grab those forceps, the little thing that looks like pliers. That's the one. While we hold the bones in place, you twist those wire ends, just like you would on a fence post. Not too tight, that silver wire won't take much pressure. . . . There, that's enough."

Monte wiped the sweat from his forehead with his sleeve. His back was already aching as he leaned over the body of his friend. He did whatever Doc told him. Twice, he twisted the little wire too hard and it broke. Doc cursed bitterly and rewrapped the bone.

At last it was finished, the muscles laid back in place, stitches rejoining the flesh.

"I'll just have to wrap it good," Doc said, "and try to keep him still until the incision begins to heal. If we can keep it from getting infected for a few days, maybe I can put a cast on it." He arched his back and stretched his arms to relieve the strain he had been under.

"Do you think it will work?" Monte asked.

"No," Doc Jacobs muttered, "the leg will probably get gangrene from that wire and I'll have to cut it off anyway."

"At least you tried," Monte said and arched his own back. "I'll give you credit, Doc, you tried."

"I didn't see much choice," Doc said and smiled at the old cowboy for the first time. "Would you really have shot me, Monte?"

"It's better you don't know," Monte said and turned toward the office door. "Some of us will be back to see how he's doing in an hour or so."

As the door closed behind the old cowman, Mrs. Miller

said, "I don't think he would really have shot you, Doc. Down deep, that old man is a decent human being."

"Well, Mrs. Miller, I'd not have taken that chance in a million years. That independent old coot is not the kind to fool with, not when he has a cocked pistol pointed at you, anyway. I've known Monte ever since I came to this country and I've never known him to back down an inch on anything. They tell me he shot two outlaws who tried to kill Mr. Major years back. There were some tough hombres around here in those days when the Lincoln County war and Billy the Kid was gettin' famous."

"Well," Mrs. Miller said as she made ready to take Vance to one of the rooms, "maybe Monte carries his loyalty too far."

"You can't be too loyal, Mrs. Miller," Doc assured her. "But, you can be loyal to the wrong people or cause. Monte knows where he stands and his loyalty is returned by every member of the Major family."

CHAPTER 2

IT was not often the Major clan gathered anymore in the old family house on Third Street in Sundown. When the old folks had lived there, it was almost a weekly event for some or most of the family to gather there. The comfortable old adobe home now belonged to Becky, the youngest of the family and the one who had cared for their aged parents during their last illnesses. Becky had been the only girl still single, and it had seemed only right that she look after the parents. When they died, the home had gone to her.

Today, the whole family gathered at the old house again. Becky had been up early and had spent all morning on the dinner. Helen Carlson, her oldest sister had gotten there an hour before mealtime. Helen was a much bigger person than the slender Becky. She was also much more forward, ready to speak out on any subject, usually in a humorous manner. Becky was the quiet one of the girls and by far the prettiest. Her golden hair set off the deep brown eyes that had turned many a man's head, but none had so far gotten beyond taking her to a social function or two.

"Liz and Stan should be here soon," Helen said. Liz was the middle sister. "I doubt Beth will come. She's too uppity for us plain folk."

"Maybe she'll come this time," Becky said with hope in her voice. "I took her for a drive last week and she seemed to enjoy that. She was very nice about it."

"Sure she was. You hitched up the horse, went by for her, took her where she wanted to drive, not where you did. Then, you did a few errands for her on your way home, dropped her off, unhooked the team, and put them up by

19

yourself," Helen said with a hearty, knowing laugh. "All the while, her majesty sat there and enjoyed herself and didn't soil a finger."

"Oh, Helen! Beth is not all bad," Becky said defensively.

"She's the worst thing that ever happened to Harvey. Why he didn't marry Hazel is more than I'll ever know."

"Hazel is still carrying a torch for him, poor thing."

Liz came with her husband and daughter, all carrying provisions for the meal.

"Brought the rolls and a cake," she said gaily. "I was going to bake some pies but just didn't get around to it."

"Cake is plenty for this crew," Helen said in the direct way she had, somewhat like Vance but less abrupt. "I brought a cake, too, and I'll bet Becky made a chocolate one to take to Vance."

"You're right," Becky said as she took the rolls from Liz.

There was a strong family resemblance between Helen and Liz. Both had brown eyes and brown curly hair. Liz was much shorter and smaller than Helen, her hands and face displaying the fact she worked hard. Her husband Stan Howard was a farmer and she helped by raising the pigs, chickens, and a few sheep, besides helping in the field when he needed it.

"Ellen, go find Susan and Little Harvey but remember to play nicely," Liz told her daughter. "Harvey and Beth here yet?"

"Princesses don't often mix with us common folk," Stan said, as he moved past the women toward the dining room. "Frank here, Helen?"

"He had to work at the store this morning; he got in a couple of loads of corn or something. He and the boys will be here for dinner."

At noon, they gathered in the large dining room. Two tables were set, the big oak table for the grown-ups and a smaller one for the children. Harvey, the tall, handsome, dark-haired brother came just as the rest sat down to eat. His wife wasn't feeling too well so he had to come alone. It was instantly plain that Harvey was the apple of his sisters' eyes, as they all made over him and hung on his every word.

Harvey was a great story teller and he entertained them all throughout the meal. He had recently been to Santa Fe and had some delightful tales of politics in the capital. After the cake had been served, the children, led by Helen and Frank's two boys, who were the oldest, went outside to entertain themselves. The three sisters cleared the table and Harvey passed cigars to his two brothers-in-law.

Frank Carlson was a tall, thin Swede. He smoked his cigar in the quick puffs of a man who seldom smoked. The women stacked the dishes in the kitchen and came back to sit at the table so they could take part in the conversation.

"Well, what's the latest on Vance?" Harvey asked, smoke curling around his handsome face. "I haven't seen him since Friday."

"Doc Jacobs says he thinks maybe the foot will heal, after all. It will probably always be stiff but he says it's doing better than he had ever hoped it would," Helen said. "I talked to him this morning. Did you know Monte threatened to shoot him if he tried to amputate that foot?"

"The heck!" Frank exclaimed.

"That's what Doc said. I guess he thought it had been crushed so badly he couldn't save it, but Monte had promised Vance he would not let him cut it off. Doc claims Monte threatened him with a gun."

"Well, I'm glad he did!" Becky said. "Vance would never have forgiven them if they'd cut it off. We owe Monte another vote of thanks."

"Doc says he thinks Vance should go to Ojo Caliente in a week or two and soak that foot in the hot mineral baths. Doc says sometimes that really promotes bones healing and keeps them from getting so stiff," Helen went on. "We know it will be months at least before Vance can go back to the ranch."

"Can Monte look after things?" Liz asked.

"He probaby can—with some help from the rest of us. We're lucky in some ways," Harvey said easily. "Having to sell all the cattle when Dad died hurt like heck at the time, but at least there's not much to do until the place gets restocked."

"All that empty grass is what bothers me," Becky said. "Vance has been worried to death about that, too. He's afraid our neighbors will move in on us."

"That's a real worry, all right. Dad worked himself to death building up that ranch but most of it is government land, open range. We really don't own it and now that we've got no stock to hold it with, it's mighty tempting to some folks," Harvey admitted.

"It will be much more tempting now that Vance isn't there. They all respect him," Liz said. "If Vance goes to Ojo Caliente and they know he's not even in the county, things will get worse."

"How soon will the cattle Vance bought be here?" Stan asked.

He immediately wished he hadn't spoken. In-laws did not discuss Major family business.

"Not for a couple of months at least," Becky said. "He contracted them from a rancher near Amarillo who insisted on wintering them. Vance got them at a good price but couldn't get delivery until this spring. I wish we hadn't had to borrow the money from Carl Farr. That's what really worries me. We had to put the ranch up for security on that note, and we could all lose our part of the ranch if anything goes wrong. Despite Harvey's connections I don't trust Carl Farr."

"What were they running the mares for, anyway?" Helen asked, changing the subject.

"Juan was to start breaking those three-year-olds," Becky said. "Those mares are always such a hard bunch to corral."

"Well, Harvey, I guess you'll have to keep your eye on things if Monte can't handle it," Liz said, eyeing her brother. "The neighbors won't move in on you."

"Hold on a minute," Becky said. "We all asked Vance to come back and run the place when Dad got sick. He'd never have come back if Harvey had not been settled in his job as sheriff. You know he always felt we looked up to Harvey over him. If Vance thought Harvey was going back to the ranch even for a short time, you know what he would do. Just leave again."

"That's true," Helen agreed. "If Harvey had wanted to come back to the ranch, Vance would still be in Arizona. We all assured Vance that Harvey would stay in his job and Vance would run the ranch. I don't think we can change that now. If Harvey moves to the ranch and gives up his job while Vance goes to Ojo Caliente, Vance will keep right on going and never come back."

"You may be right, Helen. He went to Arizona because he thought Mom and Dad and all of us wanted Harvey on the ranch more than him. He always seemed to feel it was no place for him while Harvey was there." Liz shrugged her thin, work-worn shoulders. "If we want Vance to come back to the ranch after going to Ojo Caliente, we've got to think of some way to hold the place together without Harvey moving out there. Do you agree, Harvey? Besides you've worked so hard to get elected, it wouldn't be fair at all to ask you to quit now."

Harvey nodded his head and smiled through the smoke halo. Harvey Major knew in his own mind he could run the ranch, but it would mean giving up the ambitions he had that made him leave the ranch in the first place. Then there was Beth—the woman he loved and admired most of all. She would never happily move to the Major ranch and live under conditions there. She had been so glad to move to town from her parents' ranch when she married Harvey. And her parents had the biggest and finest ranch home in the country. No, if he went back to the ranch, he could kiss his happy home good-bye. Harvey Major at least knew where he stood at home and the limits his wife set. He was free to pursue any ambition he had as long as his wife had the home she wanted and a Mexican woman to keep it clean.

"I'm afraid I have to agree, girls," Harvey said slowly. "I wouldn't mind quitting and going back to the ranch but Beth wouldn't like it and wouldn't move out there with me. I am afraid, too, Vance would leave again, no matter what assurances we gave him that he was welcome. About all I can do is to try to help out if the neighbors push in." He shook his head almost sadly. "There's not a lot I can do legally, even then. It is mostly government land and they have about as much right to it as we do. We've kept them off by running our own cattle on it and just being tough enough that they were afraid to take us on. You know Dad fought Indians, outlaws, and neighbors all his life to hold that land. He kept the neighbors off mainly by buying up the water holes and always being there to run off any stray stock."

"Well, maybe Stan or Frank . . . ," Becky started to suggest.

"Stan and Frank are good men, but needless to say neither of them know from nothing about the ranch," Helen said positively. There was no doubt in her voice. "If we can't have Harvey go back, I guess it will be up to you, Becky. You know more about the ranch than any of us because you have been going out there every summer. You've also got no other real responsibilities."

"What about Little Harvey and Susan?" Liz asked. "After all, Becky is taking care of them."

"They can stay with me until school is out," Helen said firmly. "Maybe I'll come out to the ranch this summer with them and help cook. I can't ride anymore like Becky can but I can cook. Mom and Dad never let any of us ride astride like Becky does, anyway. We always had to have proper divided skirts or ride sidesaddle."

"How about Frank and the boys?" Liz asked.

"We'll get along," the slow, easygoing Swede assured them. "Helen is usually cooking for the church or somebody in place of us anyway."

"Frank, you haven't missed a square meal since we've been married," Helen admonished him. "Look at the paunch you're starting."

"Well, I guess it is up to you, Becky," Harvey said. "I see no other way."

The pretty, slender woman's dark brown eyes looked around the table. She loved the ranch and loved to ride, but she didn't feel capable of the responsibility of actually running the place. Becky knew how much the ranch meant to the family. Her father and mother had been true pioneers on that land. She realized it meant more to Vance and herself, perhaps, than the others. Vance had quit a good job as foreman of a big ranch in Arizona to come back and take over when their father got sick. His wife had died only a few months before.

She had always felt somewhat ashamed, too, that the family had always seemed to favor the older son—she knew Vance had always felt he had to play second fiddle to Harvey. Even though he had come back when asked, Vance seemed always afraid they would turn to Harvey in case of trouble—not letting him run things his way. Perhaps she understood Vance's feelings better than the others did. But, could she actually handle the pressure of running the ranch?

"I doubt the neighbors will be much afraid of me," she said, her voice showing a little apprehension.

"At least you are a Major," Harvey said. "They will know that one of the family is there and not just hired hands. The name will mean something and I am sure your judgment will be better than Monte's. He's an old fire eater but someone should be there to keep him from going off half cocked. I'll help you all I can."

"I wish Monte were twenty years younger," Becky said. "He must be at least sixty-five, maybe seventy."

"He's all of that, but a more loyal man never lived. With him and Juan, you'll have two good men you can really count on. Bud Jarvis is not much but he is big. I know Vance has been looking for a few more men but good ones around here seem awfully hard to find right now—a year ago you could have a dozen but Vance told me he could find no one. When those cows get here, you'll have to have several more men for a time, at least," Harvey continued. "I'll try to come and give you a hand if you need me."

"All right. I don't see anything else to do. I'll see Vance this evening and go out to the ranch in the morning. We've got to keep people off that grass until our cows get here."

"It all sounded so good when Vance told us about it. I've never liked Carl Farr but he didn't seem to hesitate to loan us some money," Helen said.

"That was only because Harvey is married to his daughter," Liz said.

"Well, I wish we didn't owe Farr so much money," Helen insisted. "I'd not put it past him to put us out if he got the chance. He's done it to others and I hear he is about to foreclose on Sid Cameron right now."

"Oh, Carl will be reasonable," Harvey assured them slowly. "It's not Carl I'm worried about. It's more likely to be the little neighbors who will push in on that grass. There never was a rancher who didn't want to get bigger, always wanting the land next to him."

After the others had gone, Becky cleaned the kitchen and then packed her clothes for the ranch. She helped Little Harvey and Susan pack their things to move to their Aunt Helen's home. As Becky worked, her mind went over her problems and she felt her stomach tighten. She did not want this responsibility, and the thought of trouble with the neighbors made her sick. Harvey or Vance might fight at the drop of a hat, but she was a woman, and how could she fight in a man's world?

Yet, she knew she would do the best she could. That, too, was part of her upbringing, her Major heritage.

CHAPTER 3

THE riders eased their horses down the steep bank of the arroyo and crossed the small stream trickling along the sandy bottom. The horses' hooves dug into the trail and their muscles tightened as they climbed the far bank. Becky was behind, riding with the ease of a seasoned hand, touching her silver mounted spurs lightly to make her horse keep pace with Monte's. After they topped the arroyo the open grasslands stretched before them for miles, broken by little except scattered sage and small tree cactus and, immediately ahead, the tall cottonwoods and windmill tower alongside the low prarie ranch buildings. At the far side of the basin a dust devil swirled dirt high into the air, the whirlwind glowing red against the setting sun. The riders stopped to let their horses drink at the big wooden tank at the windmill before riding on to the corral gate.

Becky dismounted a little stiffly. It had been a long day and her body was not yet conditioned to the ranch work.

"Monte, will you take care of my horse?" she asked the white-haired cowman. "I'll start some supper."

The cowboy grunted, took the bridle reins from her hand, and led the horses inside the corral.

As she walked toward the house, her eyes glanced at the sun over the western horizon. She and Monte had gotten in a little later than usual and she wondered why the other riders had not returned before them. She could not suppress the worried look that came over her face. How she hoped they had not found where any neighbor had moved in on their grass. The fear overshadowed all her thinking.

Woodvines covered the side wall of the kitchen and the

leaves were just beginning to form. She went inside to the room that had once been the living room with its stone fireplace and that she now used as her bedroom when she and Vance's children stayed at the ranch. The house was neither big nor in any way a fancy place. Just a good, solid old ranch house. She took off her Stetson and tossed it over the spike horns of the mounted antelope head over the fireplace and shook out her honey-blonde hair. It fell down around her face and she could not resist taking the time to give it a few strokes with brush and comb. When she rode she wore a man's shirt and Levi pants. She had done this from childhood even though proper ladies frowned on such attire.

A few minutes later, in the kitchen, she started a fire in the big iron range. Between the stove and the pantry was a large box of firewood and over it was a small window looking out toward the corrals.

She dipped water from the reservoir at the end of the range into a basin, carrying it to the washstand with its high mirror near the door. When she had finished removing the stains of the day's ride from her face and hands, she carried the basin to the screen door and flipped it wide with her foot to throw the water out on the woodvines. Old Monte had taught her that habit as a child.

For a moment, as she waited for the stove to heat enough for biscuits, she went outside and stood looking out at the rolling prairie. The mournful call of the dove joined the sounds of the evening; a moment later she heard a nighthawk's zoom and the worry lines of her face softened. She had always loved evenings at the ranch. She walked to the corner of the house where she could look toward the north hoping to see some sign of the other riders. As she started to turn back into the house, a slight movement on the horizon caught her eye. On the rim of the basin a dot moved. A horse and rider.

Ringing spurs broke her thoughts as Monte walked around the corner, carrying an armload of wood.

"Rider coming," he said, stepping past her to cross the room and dump his load noisily into the wood box.

"I saw him," she said and smiled. No matter how he aged, the old cowman's eyes didn't miss much. "Wonder who it could be coming from that direction. I don't think it's Bud or Juan."

"No. They just rode in. I don't have any idea, and you ain't going to like the news Juan and Bud brought, either," Monte said. He tossed his hat on one corner of the mirror over the washstand and took the basin to the reservoir. "They found tracks of quite a bunch of cattle being driven across the west pasture near the Old Ranch. They thought they was headed toward the Big Spring."

"Did they see anyone?"

"No, only tracks. It was too late to follow them, so they came on in. It may be what we've been afraid of or it could be Anderson moving across like he sometimes does."

As he spoke, Monte rolled up his sleeves and began washing. He made bubbling sounds in the basin as he sloshed water over his face and neck. Finished scrubbing, he turned his head sideways over the basin to look at her, soapy water dripping from his chin and the point of his white mustache. Soapy water also dripped to the floor from his hand as he spoke.

"It was probably Anderson, but it's early for him and he usually lets us know when he'll cross," he said.

"He may think it didn't matter since we have no cattle on the range this year."

"That's probably right. We'll check it tomorrow."

Becky could not help the feeling of fear this news brought to her as she turned back to the stove. If only she could hold things together until Vance got back.

She began stirring the sourdough biscuits and, in spite of her anxieties, she found herself humming softly under her breath. Automatically, she made enough biscuits for an extra person.

"That rider ain't comin' from town, anyway, so it shouldn't be any more bad news," Monte added, wiping his face and hands on the towel. "About time this outfit had some good news. It might even be Anderson to let us know he was moving across."

Monte threw out his wash water and moved to the cupboard where he worked quickly to get out the tin plates and enameled cups. He slid them to their places on the oilcloth table covering. He, too, added for the extra person.

The two hired hands now came in from the corrals, each carrying an armload of kindling, which he dumped noisily into the wood box.

"Rider coming across the big arroyo," the tall, heavily muscled Bud Jarvis said. His black eyes always seemed brooding under thick lids and his dark beard all but covered his face and mouth. "Maybe just a lonely sheepherder."

"Don't recognize the horse," Juan added. "It sure ain't no sheepherder's horse."

Juan Martinez was a horseman. Monte knew Juan would notice a man's horse quicker than the man himself. From Juan's words, Monte knew the man must be riding a good horse.

"We already seen him," Monte informed them dryly. He went outside and walked slowly across to the fence to stand watching as the rider neared the windmill tank. He waited patiently until the horse had drunk, then shouted and waved his hand.

"Supper's on! Put your horse in a corral and come on in. There's hay in the loft." Juan had been right—the man's horse was a good-looking gray. Monte could tell at a glance he had been under the saddle for a good many days.

The rider waved in reply and trotted his horse to the corral where he pulled his saddle and a few minutes later walked toward the house with long, easy strides, his spurs ringing softly with each step. Monte met him at the door.

"Howdy." The old cowboy motioned for the man to come inside. "Wash up and sit."

The man was tall, thin, and sharp featured. When he removed his well-worn Stetson, his sandy hair fell down around his ears. Monte also noted that the man had shaved that morning. Monte's other observation was that the man wore no pistol, which was strange in a country where almost all riders carried some weapon. Of course, the man might have left his gun with his saddle as a polite gesture.

At the washstand, the man pulled the old, broken-toothed comb through his wet hair and carried the pan to the door, then took the seat Monte pointed out next to Bud at the rear of the table. Becky placed the platter of meat on the table and turned to dish up the potatoes. If the man was surprised to see a woman in ranch hand's clothing, he did not show it. No introductions were offered. Monte passed him the plate of meat and said, "Dig in."

Monte, as usual and from long habit, finished the meal first. The old man got up and refilled everyone's coffee cup and then sat back down and pulled the makings from his shirt pocket to fashion a brown-paper cigarette. He offered his makings across the table to the stranger. The sandy-haired man flashed a quick smile but shook his head. A little later, he took a pipe and pouch from his shirt pocket. When the pipe was lit he leaned back against the wall.

"I ain't seen you around here before," Bud Jarvis said turning toward the man, and the bench squeaked under his bulk.

"That's right," the stranger said softly in a polite and civil tone.

"Passin' through?" Bud's tone tried to disguise his pointed question.

Both Monte and the stranger's eyes went to Bud's bearded

face. "Your horse has come a long ways," Monte said. "You're welcome to rest him a few days."

"I'd like that." The man spoke with a slight Texas drawl. "I'd not want to impose."

"Sundown's only a half-day's ride," Bud suggested.

Monte snorted angrily but the stranger puffed calmly on his pipe.

Becky was the one who spoke, her voice sharp. She could assert herself on occasion and damn it, she was running things! "Bud, mind your manners. This man's welcome to stay a few days and rest his horse. That's the way it's always been and you know it."

"I'd not want to cause any hard feelings." The stranger's Texas drawl was even stronger now.

"There'll be no hard feelings," Monte said. "Miss Major is running this outfit and some folks had better damn soon remember it!"

"That's enough, Monte," Becky said, clearly in control.

Bud shrugged his massive shoulders and got up, pushing his way past the stranger, who had to lean forward to let him by. The screen door banged loudly behind him, and they heard his spurs ring as he walked around the kitchen and away from the house.

"Bud's got a nice, even disposition," Monte grunted. "He must have been brought up by a she-bear with a bellyache."

The tall stranger smiled thinly. Something about the old cowman instantly stirred in him a liking for the man.

"She must have brought up several," the man drawled slowly. "I've met his kind before."

"I'll just bet you have." Monte's faded old eyes met the young man's keen blue ones.

"They're a lot of them around," Juan said with a flash of his white teeth. "Sometimes I think too many."

Monte pushed back from the table and began gathering dishes. The stranger rose to help him.

"No need of that," Monte told him. "Becky and I are used to doing dishes."

"All the more reason to help."

"You fight over the dishes," Juan said. He took his hat from the washstand. "See you tomorrow."

"Goodnight, Juan," Becky called as the man went out the door.

"Buenos noches, Miss Becky."

Becky lit the kerosene lamp and by its light the three did the dishes in an easy silence. When they finished, Monte swept the floor and then led the way to the bunkhouse, where he showed the stranger an empty bed.

The next morning began as the sun was breaking over the horizon. Monte rolled out of bed, making enough noise to be sure no one could sleep. His feet hit the floor and he grunted loudly. After pulling on his pants he stomped his feet into his boots with much loud pounding on the floor. He whistled and snorted as he tossed his bedding around, while the others forced themselves from under their covers. It was plain the stranger had enjoyed sleeping in a bed, for he was the last to crawl from under the blankets. Juan dressed quickly and left immediately because it was his turn to wrangle horses.

Breakfast was waiting for them, as Becky had been up even earlier than Monte.

After they had eaten, Monte asked the stranger, "You decide to stay a few days?"

The man hesitated, looking at Becky.

"You're welcome," she said. "In fact, if you're hunting a job, we'll put you on."

"Thanks, ma'am, but I'm on my way to Arizona," the man said civily. "Be glad to lend a hand for a few days, though, while I rest my horse."

"We're not doing much but be glad to have you ride along with us. Got plenty of damn good horses that need riding,"

Monte said. "By the way, if you're going to be around awhile, what do we call you?"

"My name is Clint. Clint Austin."

"Fine, Clint, come on down to the corrals and I'll pick out a horse for you."

CHAPTER 4

THE two men walked to the corrals, the old cowboy pulling at his drooping white mustache and the tall, thin puncher matching his stride. At the corrals, Clint caught his gray horse and checked its legs and feet, then turned the animal into the big corral with the ranch horses.

"That's a pretty good-looking horse," Monte said as the cowboy pulled the bridle. "Ain't that the Arrowhead brand he's carrying?"

"Sure is," Clint said and smiled. The old cowman didn't miss a thing. "They tell me that's a big outfit up in Colorado. I bought the horse from a trader in Raton."

"Well, we've heard of the Arrowhead outfit, all right, even down here," Monte said. "They are supposed to have good horses, good cows, and some top riders. You ever ride for them?"

"I bought the horse in Raton," Clint repeated.

From the curt answer, Monte could tell the man wanted no more questions. The cowman grunted and went to the barn. He was back in a moment with his rope. He shook out a fairly large loop as the horses started milling around at the sight of him. The old man held the loop low down by his right knee and watched the horses move around the corral. The rope flashed out and settled over the head of a tall, well-built bay gelding. That rope had been thrown true. Clint knew instantly the man was a horseman.

Monte led the bay to Clint and the sandy-haired cowboy slipped his bridle over the animal's head. After cinching the saddle, Clint led the horse outside the corral and turned him to each side before swinging up. The horse seemed a little nervous about a strange rider but moved out smoothly when the cowboy slacked his reins. Clint turned the horse a few times and it reined well.

Monte had not been kidding when he said the Majors had some good horses, Clint thought. Someone on this ranch knew how to train horses. Probably the Mexican, Juan Martinez.

Clint rode the horse back to the corrals to wait for the others. Juan had saddled a young, good-looking red roan. Clint watched as the man led the horse to a small, round corral. Juan twisted the stirrup and swung up. The roan immediately put his head down and bucked around the corral. Clint could tell the horse did not buck too hard but the rider was one of the most graceful he had ever seen. When the horse gave up and trotted around the corral, Juan made him stop, turn both ways, and back up. Clint now was certain Juan was the rider responsible for the well-trained horses on the Major ranch. Besides having great natural athletic ability, the rider apparently had worked many years developing his talent to train horses to cow work.

Becky came from the house, her hair up under the Stetson hat and her spurs ringing. Not the typical ranch boss, Clint thought, admiring the slender, yet full figure. He'd never seen a woman dressed like that. The few women he'd known would not be caught dead wearing a man's pants and shirt. He'd heard some existed but had always thought only in some story teller's mind.

She took the reins of the palomino horse Monte was holding for her and turned the horse against the feel of the cinch, put a rein over the animal's neck, and gathered the left rein with a handful of mane to swing up gracefully, like a cowhand.

Becky sent Bud and Juan off to see if they could find where their neighbor had driven his cattle off of their range, in case the tracks they had seen yesterday had been made by Anderson, as they hoped.

Monte turned the rest of the horses into the horse pasture and Clint watched his gray run and dodge to avoid the bites and kicks of his new playmates. Monte led the way from the ranch at a fast running walk. He had noticed Clint had not left a pistol with his saddle. Apparently the man did not carry one, but a Winchester was in the boot under his right leg.

Monte and Becky rode side by side, with Clint following closely. Clint was impressed with the responsiveness of the horse they had given him. He was also impressed with the condition of the range. For short-grass country, the feed here was excellent. They happened upon antelope, jackrabbits, and two coyotes, which spooked and ran at the sight of the riders.

"My father settled here many years ago," Becky told Clint as they rode at an easy walk. "He filed on the main ranch and later bought most of the land that has water holes and springs. We control a lot of good grass we don't own. We have some cattle coming in a few weeks, and we've been holding our breath none of our neighbors try to move in on us before then."

"You must have better neighbors than some I've known," the cowboy observed. "Or the place would already be full of cows."

"I'll admit I'm real surprised some of ours haven't tried something before this," Monte said. He liked the way Clint seemed to understand instantly what was going on. "Bud and Juan seen some fresh cow tracks along the west side of the place last evening. We'll see if they are trouble. . . . "

"The neighbors would never dream of coming in on us if either of my brothers was home," Becky said wistfully.

"We're going to be a busy bunch when those cows get here," Monte drawled, a gleam coming into his eyes. "There'll be cows, calves, and quite a bunch of yearling steers and all will have to be branded. We'll have our hands full. We could use a good hand or two," he added, looking sideways at Clint.

"Clint doesn't want to hear all our troubles, Monte." Becky sensed that the man did not wish to be involved.

Clint said nothing, and the conversation was closed for some time as they rode over the soft prairie earth. They were several miles from the ranch when they found the cattle tracks Bud and Juan mentioned.

"Looks like they came out of Cameron's pasture," Monte mused, studying the sign. "Anderson sometimes comes through there."

"They seem to be heading north, which is the way he usually circles our main ranch," Becky added, trying to build up her hopes.

They followed the tracks. It had been a large herd of cattle and it was easy to follow the trail that now led up the easy slope of the big basin. As they topped the rim, the country became rougher. Sometime later, they were moving along the foot of a long, narrow hogback, which broke away into a small basin where a spring fed a large water hole. Becky was in the lead now and suddenly pulled her horse to a stop. Monte jerked his horse behind her and stood in the stirrups.

"There's cattle at the Big Spring!" Becky said excitedly. This was what she had feared! Their neighbors knew about Vance and were taking advantage of his absence. Instantly, she felt anger swell inside her. Damn, she thought, how could she force a neighbor off their land? They would laugh at a woman. Well, by God, they had better not laugh at her! No matter what it takes, she was going to try to protect this grass, because without it their new cattle would not do well and the family would not be able to make the mortgage payment.

"Well, damn somebody," Monte swore. He spurred his horse up the side of the hogback, forcing the horse every jump up the steep, rocky slope. There was no stopping the old cowman in that mood.

"There's a lot of cattle at the spring!" he called down.

Clint watched Monte as the old cowboy stood high in his stirrups, his hand shading his eyes, still managing to hold his horse on the precarious footing. Clint had to admire the old cowboy. He could relate to the man's loyalty to his outfit.

"Looks like riders climbing the trail up the hill on the far side!" Monte shouted. He sat back in his saddle and swung his horse toward the riders.

The animal scrambled and sat back on its haunches to slide down the slope. Rocks and dirt tumbled toward the other riders and Becky and Clint had to check their mounts. Monte swung past Becky and spurred his horse to a dead run along the foot of the hogback toward the spring. Becky lifted her horse to follow and Clint forced the bay to stay close behind the woman.

As they neared the water hole, cattle spooked and fled, their tails up in fright, turning after a safe distance to look back at the riders, eyes wide and muscles tense, ready to turn and run again.

"Payne's," Monte shouted as he caught a brand. A moment later he yelled, "Cameron's, too!"

Clint saw the riders watching them from the rim of the little hill across the draw the spring was in. Monte was spurring his horse at every jump as he crossed the draw and started up the trail leading to the top of the hill. Becky was not far behind the old man and Clint spurred to keep close to her. He felt the bay begin to labor as they climbed the winding trail up the steep side of the hill. The horse was not in condition for this kind of riding. By the time they reached the top, all the horses were pulling for wind, but Monte kept spurring, his horse still digging for footing as he broke over the top.

Becky topped the hill in time to see Monte slide his horse to a stop before five well-armed men. She slowed to a trot to cover the last fifty yards, then drew her horse to a stop beside Monte.

"Get your damn cows off this range!" Monte shouted, waving his right hand defiantly. "You all know this land belongs to the Majors."

"Now, you hold on, Monte," the tall rider said, twisting in his saddle to rest his weight on one stirrup. The piercing gray eyes above the hawklike nose held no humor. "Mr. Farr said it would be all right."

"Carl Farr doesn't have a damn thing to say about this range!" Monte replied angrily. "Now, get them cows out of here!"

Becky had to admire the tough old cowboy even though she wished he would show a little more restraint. Monte set his horse straight and met the men's eyes squarely, as if there were no odds against him. He would have no chance if the men were to get rough, and his harsh words were doing nothing but making them angry.

"Take it a little easy, Monte," Becky cautioned, noting the others were now looking past them at Clint. She glanced back, too.

Clint had pulled up after he had topped the rim and turned his horse sideways to let the bay catch his wind. His left side was toward the men and they could see he had no cartridge belt around his waist; therefore, he posed no threat to them.

"Mr. Flack, you know this is our range," Becky said to the Farr foreman. "Mr. Farr certainly knows we have cattle coming to stock this grass. I can't believe he would say anything that would let Payne or Cameron move in on us."

"Under the circumstances, Carl seemed to feel it would be all right," Hal Flack said evenly. His gray eyes met hers squarely. "Carl said he would speak to Vance about it."

"Becky is running the outfit," Monte cut in curtly. "Farr could have asked her. He has no right to that grass and he knows it!"

"Maybe I misunderstood, but I thought the Majors were under some obligation to Mr. Farr," Flack said.

"Obligation, hell!" Monte bellowed. "Farr may have loaned them money but that doesn't mean he can let anyone use their grass!"

"Monte!" Becky snapped in exasperation. She turned to the two riders next to Flack. "Russ and Sid, I'm surprised at you pushing in on us. We've been neighbors and friends for years."

The red-haired Sid Cameron sighed and twisted uncomfortably in his saddle. His homely face showed how little he liked this. "I'm sorry too, Becky, but I'm also under obligation to Carl Farr and I need grass badly."

"And how about you, Russ? Vance always considered you a friend."

"Hell," the squat Payne snorted, and spat out a stream of tobacco juice, part of which did not clear his chin. "You Majors have been the big outfit around here so long you seem to think you own the whole damn world. Never done a friendly thing for any of us in your lives. When we needed help we went to Mr. Farr. He said he knew it would be all right for us to put our stock here for a few weeks until your cattle got here, and we appreciate his help."

"Russ Payne, you are a damn ingrate!" Monte snarled. "Mrs. Major helped you get born. And if the Majors hadn't helped your old man feed you, you'd've never growed big enough to eat solid food."

"Ah, that's just a story you tell to make a fellow feel little." Russ spat again over his brown chin. He shifted his squat frame in the saddle.

"Don't try to tell me it's just a story! I was there and seen it all!" Monte shouted. "I'm telling you again, Carl Farr don't own this land and he don't have any say as to what cows can run on it."

"You don't own much of it, either," Hal Flack pointed out, enjoying himself. He relished his position as foreman for the most powerful landowner in this part of the state.

"We own the water and we've used the land for years,"

Becky said, again trying to get control of the conversation. "You can't use the land without using our water. Really, all you men know this. I am surprised Mr. Farr would take it upon himself to tell anyone they can use our range without speaking to one of us."

"I told you, Mr. Farr will straighten this up with Vance or Harvey. Carl is in Santa Fe right now but he should be back in a few days," Flack said evenly. "I think we all know how big a man Carl Farr is and how close he is to Harvey. So, why not let them settle this?"

Becky saw the man's hand flash a signal to the two riders on the outside of the group. These men now moved their horses ahead slowly to where they could be close to Monte while the old man kept his eyes riveted on the Farr foreman's face.

"We ain't waitin' for anything from Farr!" Monte was shouting and shaking a gnarled fist at Flack. "You move them cows right now or, by God, we'll move them for you! Any time you want to pasture cows on our grass, you come ask like a white man!"

"Miss Becky, you had better protect this old rooster," the foreman drawled, knowing well his words would rankle Monte even more. His gray eyes took in the girl's figure and he liked what he saw. "What say you and I leave the crazy old coot here with the boys and ride up country a ways. I always wanted to be alone with a lady cowboy. I'll bet we can find something better to do than talk about cows."

Monte's face went livid with anger and his white mustache bristled as the muscles of his jaw worked. Flack had gone too far! Monte would never back down now. Becky realized then Flack had no real interest in her at the moment, he was deliberately trying to rile the old man into making a rash move, so one of his men could jump him or even shoot him and then claim self-defense. Becky's eyes flashed to the long-faced rider moving slowly toward Monte, his hand on the pistol at his side. She started to shout a warning just as the sudden, loud clicking of a swift-working rifle breech stopped them all.

The long-faced rider turned his head slightly and found himself looking down the barrel of a 30/30 Winchester held very steadily in the hands of the sandy-haired cowboy on the bay horse. Emil Watson knew the odds were too great, even though he could draw and shoot faster than most men. He relaxed the grip on the butt of his pistol and slowly lifted his hand even with his shoulder.

The man on the bay spoke in a slow, lazy drawl with the strong sound of Texas in his voice. "All you so-called Farrs lift your hands real high. Never mind holding the reins. Them horses don't look like the kind that would run off with you."

Becky saw it was now Flack's face that was colored with anger as the five riders complied with the stranger's order. Most of the foreman's anger was directed at himself for underestimating this new man. By this time, Monte had also drawn his pistol and it was aimed uncomfortably at Flack's middle.

"Now, I never thought a man should speak to a lady the way you just spoke to Miss Major, cowboy," Clint's drawl continued. "Let's see if you can find the words to apologize." When Flack hesitated the man continued. "If you would rather take a lesson on how to act like a gentleman, this old Winchester will be glad to be the teacher. You look almost smart enough to catch on in one or two lessons."

"You can just go to hell!" shouted the foreman.

He would have said more, but at the sharp crack of the rifle, his hat sailed from his head. Involuntarily, he ducked, knowing it would have been too late if the shot had been aimed lower. Aware of looking foolish, he dropped his left hand to check his horse, then lifted it quickly again. Meanwhile, the long-faced rider had thought of making a try for his gun but stopped short at the lightning-fast working of the rifle lever. Monte's pistol also swung to cover him.

"I do believe I can part your hair more in the middle than you can," Clint drawled. "Now, either apologize to the lady or I'll lower my sights a wee mite."

Hal Flack swallowed hard, not wanting to give in—even the thought galled him. However, he looked from the man with the rifle to where his hat lay some ten feet away. Even from his horse, he could see where the bullet had gone through the crown only inches above his head. He decided to comply with the rifle holder's request. "I . . . I'm sorry if I said anything to offend you, Miss Major. I guess your dress made me forget you are a lady." Flack ground out the words, hating both himself and the man with the rifle.

"Well, I guess that's as close to a real apology as you can expect from ignorant folks with no upbringing," said Clint.

Even though angry, Hal Flack was a cool, thinking man. The stakes were high and the way this was turning out bothered him more than he could afford to let on. The stranger with the steady rifle bothered him most of all. Hal's gray hawklike eyes took in the man's face and appearance—he would not forget this man.

"I don't know where you come from, bucko, but it might be a good idea if you was to head back that way." The foreman spoke easily now, a faint trace of amusement creeping into his voice. "You do hire some interesting people, Miss Major."

"Don't jump to any conclusions, Mr. Flack," Becky informed the man. "We haven't hired anyone."

"I'm kind of interested in this long-faced jasper you got with you, too, Flack," Monte grunted, his pistol still covering the man. "If I don't miss my guess, he's a Watson from Lincoln County. There ain't none of them good for anything but to stir up trouble. How come you'd hire that kind, Flack?"

"Maybe for protection from the kind you hire, Monte," Flack said and smiled thinly.

"I told you, we have not hired anyone," Becky stated again,

feeling she had to let them know Clint did not work for them. "This man is just spending a few days at the ranch."

"Sure, sure. Can we go now?"

"You going to take them cows with you?" Monte asked.

"No."

The old cowboy shrugged his shoulders. There was no way they could force the men to gather the cows. Keeping his pistol out and ready, he dismounted slowly. Very carefully, he went to Watson and jerked the man's pistol from his holster.

"You'll regret taking my gun, old man," Watson said angrily. "Nobody ever took my gun."

Monte glared back at him and tossed the gun toward Flack's hat. "Well," he snapped, "you at least can say you had a new experience today." He unhurriedly unarmed the rest of the riders.

"Well, you boys just go on home," he told them with a wave of his hand. "We'll take care of your cows. I'm not saying where you'll find them, but if you ride hard enough and long enough, I expect you'll locate most of them someday."

"What about our guns?" Watson asked, still glaring at the old cowboy.

"We'll give them to the sheriff. He may let you have them back . . . if you promise to be good little boys," Monte told them, dropping the last firearm onto the pile. He picked up Flack's hat and tossed it to the man, who caught it with a flashing hand. "Now, get on out of here!"

With this, Monte sent a bullet into the ground under Flack's horse and the animal lunged to the side in fright. The foreman grabbed for the horn and reins to keep from being thrown. As soon as they could gather their reins, all the riders whirled their horses. Monte sent two more shots into the ground behind them as they spurred away.

Becky watched them go, furious at Hal Flack for what he had done and for what he had said. She turned and let her glance go to where Monte was rolling the pistols in his slicker and tying it securely behind his saddle.

She was still a little angry at Monte, too. If he had just held his temper a little and had not kept pushing Flack, she might have been able to handle the situation without it getting out of hand. At the same time, she was thankful he had not been hurt. Those men had plainly been pushing and the man called Watson had intended harm. They had deliberately tried to provoke Monte in order to have an excuse to jump him. Clint Austin had probably saved Monte's life.

"That was mighty timely interference, Clint," Monte was saying as he gathered his reins and prepared to mount. "That Watson jasper had me boxed, but I was so mad I hadn't even noticed him until you stopped him. I think he was going to draw on me from the side."

"It sure looked that way to me. I don't like his looks," Becky added. "He was awful anxious to use that gun. I never saw him before but if he really is one of the Watsons from Lincoln County, he's a hard case, sure enough."

She swung her horse around to face the cowboy on the bay, who now sat quietly with his hands folded on the saddle horn. His keen blue eyes met hers and a grin flashed across his thin face.

"Thanks, Clint," she said softly, "for sticking up for a poor working girl you don't even know."

"I was some worried about this horse," Clint said easily and moved up to join them, ignoring her remark about herself. "I didn't know what he would do when I shot off him."

"Let's get them cows movin'!" Monte growled as he pushed his horse past the others toward the trail. "It's already late."

They rode back down the trail to the water hole. It took some time to bunch the cattle and start them west. It was now midafternoon and the sun was a flaming ball hanging above the horizon. They pushed the cattle directly toward the sun. Normally, cowmen drive cattle slowly so as to keep them in as good condition as possible. Now, following Monte's lead, they pushed the animals as fast as they could force them to go. It was after darkness had settled over the country that Monte decided they were well off Major range. They had seen no sign of the riders.

There was no moon to guide them on the way home. Monte led the way, standing in his stirrups, his horse at a long, swinging trot. Becky followed directly behind him with Clint bringing up the rear. At times, Clint could barely make out the erect figures ahead of him and he marveled that a woman could put in a day like Becky had. He was a seasoned rider and even he was tired to his very bones. They had hardly stopped since leaving the ranch that morning. Yet, Becky had shown no tiredness, neither had she asked any favors.

He guessed the neighbors were pushing in on the Major range because they felt a woman could not push back. After what he had seen today, he was sure this woman would try, no matter what. She deserved help. There had been a time when he would have enjoyed nothing more than helping this girl stand up to her neighbors. The temptation was there and he felt it pulling him but he shrugged it off. This was definitely not the time; he had to consider the risks he would take. If ever there had been a time in his life to avoid trouble, this was it. He wondered what Hal Flack would try to do to him for having stopped his play this afternoon. If he read Flack correctly, the man was not one to take such things lightly, and Clint Austin seldom read a man wrong.

Becky was tired, and at times had to grit her teeth. Monte had to be made of rawhide, for he never seemed to feel any need to slacken their pace. The fierce pride of the old man would not let him slow down or give excuses to his advancing age. In one way, she was glad Vance was in town. He would have been worried sick when they had not ridden in by sundown. In other ways, how she wished she could have turned all this responsibility over to her brother. This just wasn't the way she wanted to live. She loved the ranch as much as or more than any of the family, but she hated fighting.

She wondered, too, about the man who rode silently behind her. He had defended her. Of course, had he known who Hal Flack was, or about the man called Watson, he might not have taken a hand. Knowing Flack as she did, she did not think the man would ever forget Clint had gotten the best of him. If the opportunity presented itself, Flack would make Clint pay for humiliating him.

Clint Austin? When he had spoken to Flack, his voice carried authority. They all recognized it. She had known a lot of drifting cowboys over the years, but few of them would have done what this man had done today. Clint seemed so typical of the drifting cowboys she had known at the ranch, yet there seemed something different about him. She could not put her finger on just what it was but it was there. They had all felt it when he spoke from behind that Winchester.

Her arm ached and the back of her legs felt dead from the steady, jarring trot. She changed hands on the reins and horn to relieve some of the strain. She knew from experience Monte would not slow down until he reached the ranch. He would not walk or lope the horses, either, for Monte always said the trot was the natural gait for a horse to cover a lot of ground. The only thing that mattered was to go as easy as possible on the horse you rode so he would be there if you really needed him. It was of no consequence if the rider became tired.

Becky's body was tired but her mind kept working. The neighbors were actually pushing in. Had Farr told Russ and Sid to move in on them? If he had, why? The man surely knew they needed the feed they had. She even wondered if Flack had taken it upon himself to tell them to move in. She did not know the Farr foreman well, but had heard enough to know he was respected as a good cowman—rough and a hard driver. Maybe he had ambitions of his own.

CHAPTER 5

IN the bunkhouse that night, Monte told Juan and Bud what had happened and how Clint had backed him up.

"If you want a pistol, Clint," Monte said as he finished his story, "I've got one I'll give you. It ain't new but it shoots right good."

"No thanks, Monte," the cowboy said with a smile. "I can get into enough trouble without carrying a gun. Hell, a man I once knew shot off his big toe trying to make a fancy draw with one of them."

"Well, I just hope you don't live to regret what you did today." Monte sighed as he sat on his bed and unbuttoned his shirt. "Those men could cause you trouble. If you have made up your mind not to take the job with us, I'd suggest you give them a wide berth when you leave this country. Hal Flack won't forgive you." The old cowboy stood up and used the bootjack to pull his boots. "Those boys can play rough if they ever get the upper hand with an unarmed fellow."

"From what I hear, that Watson is a real mean man with a gun," Bud Jarvis put in. "The story floating around is that he's a slick gunman from Lincoln County. There's a lot of real bad ones in that county. I hear Flack brought him in to add some weight to his crew in case the Bennetts or some of them other badland boys get much handier with a running iron."

"Well, I'm sure he's a man to watch," Monte said, then grunted and rolled into his bed.

Clint shrugged his thin shoulders and crawled into his own bed. He was too tired to really care who Watson was or what he could do. He wondered if the girl at the house could possibly be any more tired than he was. Well, a few days of this and he would be glad to ride on. He knew he had to leave before he became involved with these people and the troubles he could see they were heading for. Yet, it galled him to think anyone would harm anyone as pretty as Becky.

Clint spent two more days riding circle with Monte and Becky. Sometimes he rode for a few hours with Juan but Becky never would pair him with Bud.

When they were alone, Becky and Monte talked about the silent man who had spent these days with them. Clint seemed to fit right in with whatever they were doing, pleasant and willing to ride an extra mile or two to check some part of the pasture. He did anything they asked, or anything he thought needed doing. The man was extra quiet, at times riding with them for several hours without saying a word. This seemed natural to his nature. They were used to having a quiet man with them, for Vance Major had always been the silent type.

On the evening of the third day they got back to the ranch and found Frank Carlson, Becky's brother-in-law, waiting for them. He told them their cattle were coming on the railroad in just two days, several weeks ahead of schedule.

In the bunkhouse after supper, Monte found Clint packing his belongings in his war sack, as the cowboys called the canvas bag they carried their possessions in when traveling from ranch to ranch or on roundup.

"Guess I'll be pulling out in the morning," Clint said as Monte stopped beside him. "I'm obliged to you folks for the food and letting my horse rest up."

"You earned it," Monte answered gruffly. "Sure you won't change your mind and hire on for a while?"

"I think not. I always wanted to see that tall cactus in Arizona."

"I guess it does grow tall. Vance spent several years down there," Monte told him. "He married a girl down there but none of us ever saw her. She died after their second child was born. He sent the two children up here for Becky to take care of and stayed down there until just before Mr. Major died."

The old cowman shuffled his boots a little, not sure if he should continue.

"Becky's done a lot for Vance. 'Course she was the only one without a family and she has the Major's house in town. The ranch went to all five of the children; there's two girls besides Becky. Anyway, they all wanted Vance to come back and run the place, which was working out just fine until he got hurt. The other brother, Harvey, has a good job but some wife and in-law problems. Not that Harvey couldn't run the outfit, mind you, he's a good cowman, but the family knew Vance would never come back if Harvey was in charge of things. So, it fell to Becky to try to hold the place together until Vance can get his leg healed enough to come take over."

"It's no job for a woman," the sandy-haired cowboy observed in that slow civil way he had. "Not with the kind of neighbors you've got." He tossed his sack on the bunk. "I'm sure, though, you can hold things together, Monte—you were sure a fire eater when we met Flack the other day."

Monte shrugged his shoulders, feeling he had talked too much. The Majors would not appreciate his having told all their personal history to a stranger. They seldom asked for help on this ranch but Clint was a top hand, and if the Major ranch ever needed a few hands, it was now. Since Clint had chosen to move on, Monte would not ask him again to ride for them. No Major ever begged help from anyone.

Clint got up and walked out of the bunkhouse. The evening air was soft and the moon was up. He could see the sage-covered prairie stretching silver colored to the horizon. The windmill creaked pleasantly as it lifted water to the tank. From high above came the sounds of the nighthawks as Clint walked slowly to the corrals. He leaned his arm over the top rail and watched the night horse slowly circle the corral. His arms folded underneath his chin, he was thinking about things that might have been and some things that had been.

It was not often you met people like Becky Major and old Monte, either. They were people he could like a lot. He felt a strong urge to stay and help them, for they certainly had a big job on their hands, too big for any woman to handle. To do so would mean taking a hand in their trouble. This simply was not the time, he told himself again. Tomorrow he would ride on. . . .

Clint turned to lean back against the fence and reached for his pipe and tobacco. A huge figure stood only a few yards from him.

"You walk real quiet for a big man, Bud," Clint said, trying to show as little surprise as possible. Damn, he thought, I'd better not get careless. He let his hands drop to his sides.

"I learned from an Indian," Bud mumbled. "Monte told us Becky offered you a job."

"That's right."

"You going to take it?"

"No, not that I see it concerns you."

"I just want to make sure you make the right decision," the bearded man said. "If you was to make the wrong one, I'd have to change your mind."

"Well, now ain't that interesting," Clint observed, stepping away from the fence. "Just how do you plan on doing that?"

"It's better you don't tempt me to find out, fella. I don't like your ways none at all. We don't know nothin' about you except you pulled a rifle on Hal Flack. That's bound to cause trouble. He's foreman for Carl Farr, and Carl Farr is the big frog in this puddle."

"You're not very bright if you think a man like Flack will leave you alone as long as you're nice to him," Clint stated evenly, and again the strong Texas accent had come into his voice. Sometimes it was entirely absent. "I don't think I made any trouble for this outfit and surely none for you."

"Well, are you staying or leaving?"

"I had planned to leave but I might just change my mind. I don't like threats."

Bud Jarvis lunged at him. The big man moved fast and caught Clint's shirt just below the throat with his left hand, and swung his huge right fist, clublike, at Clint's face. Clint Austin proved to be deceptively swift. He jerked away, leaving part of his shirt in the man's hand, and managed to duck under the blow. At the same time, he struck a solid blow to the pit of Bud's stomach. The blow hurt and Bud knew this man had been in a fight before.

The big man rushed Clint again, using his bulk like a ram. The lithe cowboy dodged and ducked and still managed to land several hard blows to Bud's bearded face, as well as his soft middle. However, with each rush he had to give ground. Bud was pushing him back toward the corral fence. Clint did not want to be pinned against the fence and he tried desperately to slip around the big man. Bud was just as determined not to let his prey escape and to keep what advantage his size and tremendous strength gave him. Slowly, Bud forced the hard-hitting puncher back. Clint was unable to maneuver as he had because of the fence. Bud managed to get one of his looping blows partly past Clint's guard. Although the blow did not land full force, it still had enough power and weight behind it to knock Clint to his knees. Bud was on him instantly, riding him down. His head hit against a corral pole and he fell flat, Bud's big hands pushing his face into the soft dirt.

Bud was too heavy for Clint to roll off his back, the man's grip too strong to break. Clint brought his feet up, driving his spurs against the big man's back. Bud grunted but hung on, shoving harder on Clint's neck and twisting those huge hands with all his strength. Dirt was now in Clint's mouth and nose and he realized the man was trying to kill him. In desperation, he brought his feet up again with all his strength. This time, the man's big hands loosened slightly and Clint pushed up with all his might. At last, Bud rolled from his back.

Both men scrambled to their feet, Clint gasping for his

breath and spitting mud from his mouth. Bud swung first, just as Clint was starting a blow. The hamlike fist caught Clint solidly on the side of his face. Something exploded in his head and Clint went sprawling in the dust again. He tried desperately to catch himself against the fence but his fingers could not get a grip on the poles.

Bud stepped forward and was in the act of lifting a big foot to kick the fallen man in the face when a gnarled old hand grasped his thick shoulder and pulled him off balance. Monte stood beside the big puncher, his pistol held low but centered on Bud's middle. "What the hell is going on here?" the old cowman demanded roughly.

"It's nothing to you, Monte," Bud growled. He was angry but he respected the gun in the old man's hand. "This is a personal thing just between us. I don't like him and I expect he doesn't like me."

"Bud, someday you're going to beat up the wrong man," Monte told the young giant in a matter-of-fact tone. "This may have just been the time. The Majors won't like you doing this to a man they invited to spend some time."

"You ain't runnin' this outfit, Monte. As long as there's only a woman running things, I'll work over any damn puncher I want. This waddy won't push me again, I'll bet you on that."

"Personally, I don't care if he puts on a gun and kills you," the old man told him.

"You scare me bad, Monte. I don't care how many guns he puts on, I'll take care of him." Bud stomped off toward the bunkhouse.

Clint was slowly pushing himself to a sitting position, his arms aching from the strain of lifting his body. He spat and his head began to clear a little. He spat again. No matter how many times he spat, he seemed unable to clear the dirt from his mouth. Monte helped him to his feet and walked beside him to the bunkhouse. The old cowman washed and cleaned the bruised face and Clint crawled silently into his bed. He ached so much it was some time before he could drop off to sleep.

Morning found Clint's lips puffed and a dark, angry bruise pushed outwardly under his left eye. He tried to smile at Monte as the old cowboy stomped into his boots but it hurt too much. Pride made him take the pain of shaving. As he looked into the cracked mirror he noticed several cuts on his face. Leaning forward, he got close enough to the mirror to see them clearly. They were all in the shape of a small X. Bud must wear a ring that had caught him just right to make those marks.

Bud did not bother to speak as he dressed and left the bunkhouse. It was his turn to wrangle the saddle horses.

Becky gave a startled exclamation at the sight of Clint's face as he entered the kitchen. Clint was plainly embarrassed. He tried again to smile and she could tell it hurt him to make the effort.

"What in the world happened?" she demanded.

"That's a tough door Monte has on the bunkhouse," he managed to drawl. He immediately began helping Monte put the dishes on the table.

"Now, I want the truth. What happened?" Becky would not be put off.

"Bud," Monte grunted the one word.

"Why in the world?"

"I don't rightly know, Becky. Bud jumped him down at the corrals last night. He'd have done a lot worse if I hadn't heard them and gone to see what was going on. I guess I should have shot Bud, but I didn't!"

"Well, I'll have no more of this!" Becky knew Bud would never have done such a thing had Vance been there. It made her furious that men had no fear of a woman boss.

"Forget it, ma'am," Clint advised. "Some men just don't hit it off. Bud and I would never get along."

"Well, I'll get rid of him!" Becky snapped. "You were our guest. . . . Bud is fired!"

"Good riddance," said Monte. He had let Bud stay just because they had not been able to find other riders.

"Don't do that," Clint pleaded. "I'm not really hurt. I'll be gone, and you will still need the man."

"We need riders, yes, but not that bad," Becky informed him curtly. "I don't like this."

"Well, if you would take some advice from a man you don't know, I'd not cut off my nose to spite my face."

This was good advice and she knew it. At the same time, the urge to fire Bud was very strong. Could Clint be to blame? She turned this thought aside. He had stood up for her. Shouldn't she do the same for him?

As soon as breakfast was finished she called Bud aside and pointedly gave the big man to understand she would not tolerate another such incident. There was no way the man could misunderstand the blunt language she used.

"If you don't like to work for a woman, you just say so. I'll get your check," she concluded.

Bud looked away and said nothing.

Becky went to her room and made ready to go to town with Frank Carlson. It seemed wonderful to be wearing women's clothes again. She smoothed her skirt and glanced sideways in the mirror. She wondered what Clint would think—he had never seen her in a dress. She could not help but be a little pleased with what she saw in the mirror.

After Frank and Becky had left in the big wagon, the men saddled their horses as they were all going to town for the cattle. Clint brought his sack of belongings from the bunkhouse. His gray horse was well rested from days of good grass and doing nothing.

Clint rode leisurely, with Monte leading Becky's palomino. She would ride with the men the next day, helping with the cattle. Once in town, Clint went first to the barber shop to get a haircut. He met Monte on the street and the old cowboy invited him to have a drink at one of the saloons. Neither man was a heavy drinker and they soon went to a cafe and ordered a good meal. They spent most of the afternoon playing pool with a lonesome cattle buyer who won most of the games. Something kept telling Clint he should move on—yet another side of him wanted to wait.

"I guess I'd better see if they have a room at the hotel," Clint said as the two men came back out to the street. "It's too late to start anywhere today."

"I already got one," Monte grunted. "It's got two beds. You're welcome to one."

"Thanks. I'll pick up a few things at the store and see you at the hotel in about half an hour."

Monte waved his hand and started up the street toward the Majors' house. Maybe Becky would have found a few more riders or have some news about Vance.

Clint sauntered across the dusty street to Fisher's General Store, which looked to be the only mercantile in town. As he swung the door open and stepped inside he almost bumped into Hal Flack. The tall, hawkish-looking man had been in the act of reaching for the door handle when Clint opened it. For a second, the Farr foreman stood there, his right hand outstretched as though to shake hands. Flack quickly dropped his hand to his side as the surprised look on his face changed to one of amusement. Three men stood behind the Farr foreman. Two of them had been with Flack the day on the hill. The third man, with close-cropped iron gray hair, hazel eyes, and ruddy complexion, was one Clint had not seen before. The man was no cowpuncher. Clint knew the man was to be reckoned with—plainly a man of importance.

"Afternoon," Clint said pleasantly and started to move past the group. He wanted no trouble.

"Hold on just one minute," one of the men with Flack spoke. It was the long-faced, hard-eyed rider, Emil Watson. He stepped in front of Clint, blocking the narrow aisle.

"Yeah, what's your big hurry, mister?" Hal Flack asked, swinging around beside Clint. "I'd like a chat with you. From the looks of your face I'd say you tangled with someone a little bigger than you are."

Clint turned from Watson to look at Flack and the man with the iron gray hair. He watched as they examined the marks his fight with Bud had left on his face.

"Monte's got a right mean door on the bunkhouse," he drawled lazily after they had plenty of time for their inspection.

"I've heard of them doors," Flack said, smiling, and his voice seemed to hold no malice. "This is the fellow I told you about, Carl. He was with the Major outfit the other day when they gave me a bad time about Cameron and Payne putting cows on what they call Major range."

"Is he the one who shot your hat off?" asked the ruddy-faced rancher.

"He's the jasper."

Carl Farr held out his hand. Surprised, Clint held back a second, then he accepted the man's handshake. The firmness of the man's grip belied the soft appearance.

"I'm Carl Farr."

"Austin's my name," Clint responded.

"Glad to know you, Austin. Any man who can get the best of my outfit like you did is to be appreciated. Mind saying where you're from?"

"Why, Texas, of course. I'd have thought you would have heard of Austin, Texas," Clint drawled with his strongest Texas accent. He did not smile as he spoke and he was not too sure himself why he had spoken out that way. Perhaps it was just because these men were pushing Becky Major. Damn, he would have liked to help that woman, and he did not like having people question him if they had no cause. He hadn't been in Texas for years, but it was none of their business.

A steely look came into Carl Farr's eyes and the lines along his jaw set firmly. He was not used to being spoken to in this manner. Carl Farr had no use for impudent cowhands. Yet, he had to begrudgingly admit this cowboy was his own man.

"Are you riding for the Majors?" the rancher asked in a deceptively soft tone.

"I stayed at their ranch a few days," Clint drawled, the Texas accent strong in his voice.

"You still did not say if you are riding for them."

"Not at the moment," the cowboy told him. Farr let a satisfied smile cross his face. It faded when the man added softly, "At the moment I'm standing here answering silly questions."

"You may find yourself in something you can't smart-talk your way out of," Flack advised, plainly irritated, yet amused. "Mr. Farr means to know who is on the Major payroll, especially since you cut yourself into a big hand the other day. I'd advise a straight answer."

"Of course. Yes, sir. This is as straight as I know how to put it. As far as I'm concerned, I don't see it is any of your damn business. I'm getting real tired of people trying to tell me who I can work for around here. If you want to go to Miss Major like gentlemen and ask her politely, she might tell you who was working for her, if she thought you ought to know." As the cowboy spoke, he could not hide the little smile on his bruised lips but his eyes did not smile. They were blue ice.

"Well, don't be so huffy. I've got no intention of cutting in on your precious freedom. Just curious if you were working for the Majors or whether or not you were available for other employment. I am not in the habit of hiring men who are already working for a neighbor." The rancher had open disgust in his voice now. Clint knew he lied as he spoke, he would bet the man would hire anyone he wanted. "And I do have some openings."

"I am not going to work on your outfit," Clint told the man without hesitation.

"Then you are riding for the Majors?"

"I didn't say that. They do seem like nice people."

"Oh, they are the finest," Carl Farr assured him. "Absolutely only the finest. However, they can't offer a man much incentive or security. I'd hate to see a man of your talents being wasted. Sure you couldn't use a good job with a winning outfit?"

"No."

The one word was as blunt as Clint could make it and he made no effort to soften it.

"Well, now we know where we stand," Farr said, again speaking very pleasantly. "Let me tell you something for your own good, Austin. Our local cattlemen do not look too kindly on drifters. We've had considerable trouble with some of that kind the past few years."

"Also, after Mr. Farr has offered you a job, he will not take kindly to your changing your mind and thinking of working for some other outfit around here, especially the Majors," Flack added bluntly. "You had your chance. Ride on out of the country and we'll forget what happened the other day. Stay here and you'll regret you ever took a hand in the big boys' game."

The urge to tell them all where to go swelled in Clint's throat but he held it back, telling himself again this was not the time. He had probably already said too much. Besides, there was nothing to be gained by taking on trouble that was not his. There had been a time . . . He couldn't help but think what a difference it made when you had a real outfit backing you, too. Now, he was alone.

Clint met the men's eyes squarely a moment, then turned to walk away. The long-faced rider again blocked his path. Watson's right hand hung loose and near the gun he wore low on his right hip, tied down with a leather thong. Clint read the hatred in the man's sad eyes and judged Watson to be a gunman with an established reputation.

"You can't very well add a notch to your gun for shooting

me," the cowboy told the gunman cheerily. "Most authorities won't let you count unarmed men."

"Nobody ever took my gun away before," Watson said softly. "You're lucky I got it back."

"Oh? And, I do hope the sheriff made you promise you'd be good before he gave it back to you." Clint's bruised lips grinned and he pushed the man back against the counter so he could brush past him.

He did not look back but went to the grocery counter and began studying the supplies on the shelves behind it.

"You know something, Watson, I don't think you scare him much," Flack commented, a little laugh in his voice. "Maybe he doesn't know who you are."

"If he stays around here he's going to find out," Watson promised as they went out the door.

Flack turned on the sidewalk. "I hope he rides out of here because he could sure spoil some plans," he told his employer. "Even so, I admire his guts. He's got a lot of sand and bottom and I wish he worked for us. We sure don't need his kind at the Major ranch."

"No damn cowboy is going to spoil my plans," Carl Farr stated in that purposeful, forceful way he had. "If he rides on, that's fine. I've made it impossible for the Majors to hire any spare riders and I don't intend to let an outsider slip through. If he changes his mind, you have Bud take care of him."

"You bet, Mr. Farr."

Inside, Clint purchased a few provisions. The store was also a post office and he bought an envelope and stamp. He tore a piece of brown wrapping paper from his package and on it he wrote his name, Major ranch, Sundown, New Mexico. Nothing more. He folded the paper inside, sealed and addressed the envelope, and dropped it in the letter box. He knew the people getting it would be glad to know where he was. How he would have liked to be back at the old home ranch tonight, with friends he held so dear. He knew they would understand both his reason for wanting to help Becky and Monte and also why he could not. However, he was not about to let Carl Farr think he had been frightened by his threats. He would be damned if he would leave under threat.

CHAPTER 6

IT was still dark when Becky was awakened by the sound of knocking at the front door of the old adobe house. She shivered at the early morning chill as she slipped out of her bed and into a light robe.

"Who is it?" she called, leaving the door latched.

"Your cattle will be at the pens in an hour or less," a man's voice said from the darkness outside. "Will your crew be ready to unload?"

"Could you go to the hotel and tell Monte? Tell him I'll meet him at the pens."

"All right, ma'am."

She listened to the man's heavy tread cross the porch and the walk to the yard gate, and heard the creak of the gate as he went through and fastened it. She hurried to her room where she quickly dressed in ranch clothes. Yesterday, it had seemed so good to be wearing a dress again. Some of the town women might see her today. She knew too well what most of them thought of any woman who would wear pants and ride a man's saddle. Well, let them think what they wanted, she had a man's job to do and she dressed accordingly.

Last night she had gone over plans with Harvey, and this business had sounded simple. The big problem was lack of cowboys. Harvey was going to help at least long enough to get the cattle strung out and headed toward the ranch. Then the four of them would be on their own.

Monte had put her horse in the barn behind the house. As soon as she had dressed and eaten a cold breakfast, Becky hurried to brush and saddle the palomino. The streets were dark and deserted as she rode to her sister's house to tell Frank the cattle would soon be there. Frank would have to harness the team and drive the big stock wagon to the pens.

She did not tarry at the Carlson house, but rode to the railroad pens at the edge of town. Her riders were nowhere to be seen, and she rode to the pen where the men had put their horses the day before. When she saw Clint's gray with the others, she wondered where the tall cowboy would be going that day. It had been good to have him around, and she wished secretly he was going to help them get the cattle back to the ranch. Although he had only been around a short time, he already seemed to be a part of the outfit.

Clint had not slept well that night. He lay in bed listening to Monte's heavy breathing, and the thought of Becky Major kept running through his mind. He'd never known a woman like Becky. He knew he had no chance to win her but he could sure think about it.

It went against his nature to allow any man to push him. Bud Jarvis had beaten him to make sure he did not stay. Then, the threat from Carl Farr, either ride for the Farr outfit or get out of the country. He had never taken such threats and pushing from anyone. Under other circumstances there would have been no hesitation. In fact, there had been a time when he would have enjoyed showing Carl Farr and all of them what they could do. Even though the arguments were sound and he should ride on for his own good, Clint knew himself. He just couldn't ride out on the girl and old Monte. Not under threats. He hadn't changed that much.

He was awake when the man from the railroad came down the hall to rap on their door. Monte was also awake. While Clint lit the lamp on the small table between their beds, Monte answered the knock on the door. The old cowman swore a little at the message. He had never thought too much of these new ways of transporting cattle. To Monte's way of thinking, the Lord had given cows four legs to walk on, and the best way to move them from one place to another was to let them use their legs.

The old cowman returned to his clothes, which were piled in a heap on the chair by his bed, and quickly began pulling on his pants. Clint watched only a moment and also began to dress. Monte went out and down the hall to the room Juan and Bud shared. When he returned, he found the tall, sandy-haired cowboy dressed to leave, his war sack on the chair and his rifle in his hand.

"You leavin' this early?" Monte asked. He put on his hat and pistol before looking around the room to make sure he had not left anything. "You could sleep another hour or two and still get an early start."

"You'll need a lot of help today," Clint volunteered softly.

"You knowed that yesterday." Monted watched the man closely.

"Yeah, but to tell the truth, I'm just not quite ready to let Bud Jarvis or Carl Farr tell me who I can ride for," Clint said. "Farr told me yesterday to either work for him or ride out of the country. Guess I'm just too old to change my ways completely and let men like them push me. I'll help you get those cattle home."

"You know, I just kind of wondered if that might not be the way you'd react," Monte said. His gnarled hand went to his mustache but it could not completely hide the grin beneath it. "Glad to have the help," he said.

"Well, blow out the lamp and let's go before I change my mind again."

They had to wait for a few minutes in the lobby for Bud and Juan to join them. From the hotel, they walked the two blocks of Main Street looking for a cafe that would be open at this hour. They found none and walked on out of town to the pens where they found Becky waiting for them.

Clint caught his gray and threw his saddle on. He drew the cinches to his liking and tied the canvas sack of belongings securely behind the saddle. As usual, Bud was slower than the others and had just swung his heavy saddle on his horse when Clint spoke to him. The big man spun around at his first word.

"Bud," Clint said evenly but with a strong Texas accent, "I've decided to stay a few days and help get these cattle to the ranch and settled. If you have any objections you can bring them up now and we'll settle them."

As he spoke, Clint swung his rifle across his saddle as though starting to put it in the saddle scabbard. He held the gun for a moment, pointing in the general direction of the big man. Even in the darkness, Bud did not miss the intent.

"I already told you what I thought," he grumbled roughly, remembering what this man had done to Hal Flack with that rifle. He also recalled Becky's warning.

"Yeah, you told me," Clint drawled. "Now, I'll tell you. Leave me alone."

"You don't scare me." Bud laughed harshly.

"Then you're as dumb as you look," Monte said, for he had overheard the conversation. "While Clint is riding for the Majors, you'll leave him alone. If you lay a hand on him and he doesn't kill you, by God, I will!"

Bud swallowed whatever he had to say and moved away. A train whistle sounded and they turned to their work.

"These pens won't hold more than a few hundred head," Monte told them. "As soon as they're filled, we'll have to let the cattle out and herd them until we can get the rest unloaded. There's to be two trainloads. I sure hope they get the second one here by the time we get this one unloaded. It would be just like the damn railroad to pull in with that second train just about sundown tonight."

Frank Carlson drove up with the big stock wagon and Monte went to tell him where he wanted him to work. Becky joined them, leading her horse.

"To start with, Frank, how about you helping Clint unload the first cars," Monte instructed. "The rest of the boys and I will keep the stuff moving until the pens are full."

"Sure, Monte." Frank smiled and ambled off toward the tracks where the train crew was backing the first car toward the unloading chute.

"I thought Clint said he was leaving," Becky said to Monte.

"Guess he changed his mind. Or, maybe somebody changed it for him. He told me he met Carl Farr and Hal Flack in the store, and I guess they made it plain he either went to work for them or get out of the country. That, on top of Bud beating him up, made him want to stay and let them know they couldn't push him around. He told Bud what he would do if Bud didn't like it and I'll back him up in that."

"So will I," Becky promised frankly. So he wouldn't let Carl Farr push him? Clint went up in her opinion. She admired the man.

Frank joined Clint as the first car was backed into position to unload at the chute. It took them a few minutes to set the adjustable wings of the chute and place the ramp across to the car. They had to use a bar to force the door open. A moment later, cattle began crowding down the ramp into the pens. Then Clint checked to make sure every cow was out of the car. They pulled back the ramp and wings so the next car could be brought into position.

Frank pitched right in. He was no cowman but he was a willing worker. As soon as the second car was spotted they adjusted the ramp and wings and barred the door open. Crowded in among the cows were two calves, one of which must have been born on the train. After the cows were in the chute, Clint went into the car and carried out the little red and white bundle.

"We had better find his mama," Clint said, smiling. "I don't think he can make the trip, even in the wagon."

"We'll leave the mother and calf," Monte grunted. "We can get Banister at the livery to feed them until we can get back. He would never make this drive."

Becky and Juan soon had the mother located and separated into a small pen, where Clint carried the calf.

They unloaded two more cars without incident, then found a car with several small calves. It took them a little while this time to find the mothers.

"I'll bet them cows haven't been watered for at least two days," Monte said as he and Becky watched the cows milling and bawling around the pens. "The second train will be mostly steers. I hope they were watered. If not, these animals will be hard to hold."

"If they get into town, there will be hell to pay," Becky said with a sigh, thinking of what the town ladies would think of her riding through town trying to keep her cattle off their yards. "I wish Harvey would get here. He's supposed to help today."

"It just goes to prove you can't depend on the other fellow to look after your stock," Monte said, more sure of his opinions than ever.

"Our first water will be Martinez Lake," Becky said. "I hope we can get them there without trouble. No more help than we have, it will take a small miracle. I can just see them going through town tearing up everything looking for water."

The pens were filled with cattle. Bud Jarvis grumbled when Monte told him to help Frank with the unloading. Monte really couldn't blame Bud, as no cowboy ever wanted to work on foot when there was horseback work to be done. However, Monte wanted the best crew outside the pens holding the stock. He knew Clint would do a better job than the big Jarvis.

Clint got his horse and led it outside the pens and around to the stock wagon. He untied his war sack and laid it on the wagon seat. He mounted the gray and rode to where Becky and Juan were waiting for Monte to open the gate and turn the cattle out. The sun was just peeking over the horizon and the air was chilly.

"I'm glad you decided to stay, Clint," Becky said as Clint rode up beside her. "We do appreciate the help."

Monte had opened the big gate and the cattle were streaming out of the pens. There was some sparse grass close by but the cattle seemed only to sample this and walk on. It was plain they were in search of water.

"Let's try to keep them headed north and east, away from town," Becky instructed, moving her horse ahead.

The three riders soon found they had their hands full trying to keep the cattle headed in the right direction. Becky stationed herself between the two men and made a hand. Any time a cow moved out, she turned it back as well as any cowboy could have done. Clint almost forgot she was not just another puncher.

It was also plain Clint knew what he was doing. He seemed to anticipate just when a cow was going to make a move and had his horse ahead of her with little effort, alert to the slightest movement of the cattle, as well as the turning and pivoting of the well-trained cow horse he rode.

Two men approached from town at a high lope, one on a flashy black and white pinto. He waved at the three riders as he swung his horse toward the lead cattle farthest away from the pens. The second rider swung in behind the man on the pinto. Had it not been for the arrival of these men, the others could not have held the cattle away from town much longer.

By midmorning the last of the stock was outside the pens, and Monte and Bud rode to join those holding the herd.

"Juan and I'll take the point!" Monte called, loping past Becky and Clint. "I've sent Frank to tell Banister to take care of the stock at the pens. He'll catch up. Sorry about no breakfast, Clint. Maybe they'll settle down after a bit and you can cut back to town and get some."

"It won't be the first I've missed!" the cowboy shouted after him.

Clint dropped behind the herd to ride drag with Bud. At

first, the cattle were so glad to be out of the cars and on the move they needed little urging. Clint knew, however, it would not be long before a certain number of the cows and small calves would have to be continually pushed along. None of the calves were very old, and some of them would have to be put in Frank's wagon before they were halfway to the ranch. The wagon would only hold so many, however, and some would have to walk all the way. The mixture of cows and steers did not help matters, either, as the steers would travel faster and pull ahead of the rest unless they were held back by the point riders.

Some time later Becky came close to Clint as she rode back alongside the herd. "We'll water them at Martinez Lake in a couple of hours," she told him. "The lake belongs to Juan's family and they always let us water there. The way the cattle are acting, it's a good thing we don't have much farther to go to water."

"They're some thirsty," Clint agreed and drew his horse to stop and rest a moment.

The woman also stopped her horse beside his, and for a brief moment they sat in comfortable silence watching the cattle drift by. Then, they lifted their reins and moved away from each other.

The steers had worked their way to the front of the herd. They smelled the water of Martinez Lake. Almost as one, the leaders broke into a trot. Monte and Juan moved quickly to hold them back, and Monte waved his hat high over his head to signal the swing riders to come forward. Instantly, the tall rider on the flashy pinto spurred ahead while he called loudly and waved to the rider across the herd.

Becky had seen them and knew what it meant. She turned back and loped her horse toward the rear until she could see the two men riding drag. She drew her horse up, shouted as loud as she could and waved her hat high in the air. Clint saw her instantly and started his horse around the herd, at the same time calling to Bud.

"Up front!" he yelled.

The big man looked from Clint to the girl still waving her hat. He reluctantly lifted his horse to a trot and started around the far side of the herd.

Clint let the gray out to a long, easy lope and moved wide around the cattle toward Becky, who now turned her horse and raced toward the front of the herd. The lead steers were now pushing the other riders, trying to break through and run for the water. Becky and Clint hardly got to the front in time to help hold some of them back. A moment later, about twenty head got past Juan and one of the men from town.

"Let them go!" Monte yelled. "Hold what you can and split them up around the lake."

There was no way they could really hold them all, but they managed to force the cattle to split into small bunches, keeping all of them from getting to the lake at the same time. After a time, it became hopeless and the riders eased their tired mounts to the side. They had at least scattered the herd all around the oval of the lake where most could get to the water. The cows and calves reached the lake while most of the steers were still drinking. The cows pushed the earlier animals out into the lake so they, too, could drink. They all wanted fresher water, as the water near the shore was now churned to mud. The latecomers kept pushing the earlier ones farther out into the lake.

"Some of them are bogging down, Monte!" Clint called from where he watched from the left bank.

Becky and Monte had joined the man on the pinto, and all three now rode toward Clint at a fast trot. Juan and the other riders came from the other side toward them.

They tried to push some of the cattle back to give those in trouble room to get out, but the cattle in the back were frantic with thirst and it was all but impossible to push them away from the water.

Finally, after much shouting and cursing, the riders managed to push most of the cattle down the lake bank where the bottom seemed more solid.

"Looks like the first twenty feet is hard!" Monte shouted, turning back toward the dozen or so cows, who appeared to be stuck in the mire. "Some of them are going to drown if we don't move fast. Juan, start pulling those cows!"

Juan rode into the water and was quickly joined by the tall rider on the pinto. They rode out as far as they dared, which brought the water almost to their stirrups. The men stood in their saddles, swung their loops and caught two cows. They turned their horses, dallying ropes around saddle horns, the horses struggling for footing as the ropes drew tight.

Monte was watching intently as the horses strained against the pull. One horse was not going to be able to do it, and he rode into the water to throw a loop over the cow Juan was trying to pull from the mud. It took both horses straining their utmost to pull the struggling animal to where she could get solid footing. The cow did not cooperate any, either. She braced her legs and fought the ropes as they dragged her to dry ground. Not in the least grateful, she came out full of both anger and fight.

Clint loped his horse to where Becky was holding some of the cattle away from the troubled area.

"Hold my horse!" he called, swinging down swiftly.

She took the reins from his hand and watched him run to where Monte and Juan had gotten the cow to dry ground. The cowboy ran in close and managed to grasp the loop of Monte's rope and the old cowboy slacked off immediately. A second later, Clint flipped the loop over the cow's head. Carefully, he worked close enough again to grab Juan's loop and, a second later, slip it over her head.

Instantly, the cow turned on him, bawling in anger. Luckily, she was weakened and choked down by the ropes, as well as full of water. All this slowed her, and Clint had no trouble avoiding her rush. Monte quickly put his horse between the man and the cow as Becky rode forward to help them push the angry animal toward the main herd. After the cow had been driven a little distance from the lake, she seemed to forget the man and went off to join her sisters who were now spreading out in search of grass.

"Why not let Frank hold Clint's horse at the wagon?" Monte suggested. "Then you can stay close to him while he's taking our ropes off. Get between him and those cows as fast as you can because they will sure come out of there on the fight."

Clint was taking the ropes off the cow Juan and the man on the pinto had brought to shore, before she could lope to the wagon, leave the gray horse, and get back to the lake. Monte helped the cowboy get away from that cow and Bud drove the animal off toward the herd. Juan immediately rode back into the lake to rope another cow. A moment later, Monte's rope settled over her head and they began pulling the reluctant animal toward shore.

This cow really fought the ropes. As soon as she reached solid footing, she bellowed and bawled, bucked and kicked in her struggles against the choking ropes. When Clint tried to get close enough to her to get his fingers on one of the loops, she threw herself at him, almost knocking him to the ground. The tall man on the pinto horse expertly flipped a loop to catch her hind legs. Clint knew a roper when he saw one and the handsome man riding the pinto was an expert. The man turned his horse to the side and soon had the cow stretched out on the ground.

When Clint had the ropes off the cow's head, the man moved the pinto forward, loosening the rope on her back feet; the rope fell to the ground as the cow struggled to her feet. She was still full of fight and she charged the man on foot even though he stood quite close to Becky's horse. Becky jumped her horse to get between Clint and the cow but could not prevent the cow from turning behind her horse to come after the cowboy. Clint managed to dodge back toward

Becky's horse, going under the horse's neck as the cow charged past him.

The cowboy's foot slipped as he cut back to keep the horse between himself and the cow. Instinctively, he reached out to catch himself, and his fingers closed on Becky's leg, just above her knee. After he righted himself and loosened his grip, Clint looked up to see the startled expression on the woman's face.

Clint had done the only thing he could to save himself from falling. He had merely caught hold of the first thing his hand had come to. She knew he had not meant to grab her. However, the firm grip on her leg had been that of a steel spring and, as she drove the cow away, she could still feel the places his fingers had been. In spite of herself, she felt her face grow warm. A lot of women might like to have a man touch their leg but she had not been raised that way. No man had ever touched her leg before, accidentally or otherwise.

As soon as Bud took the cow, Becky turned to lope back to be ready to help Clint with the next one. From then on, she worked expertly, always putting her horse between him and the cows, maneuvering her horse to protect the man on the ground at all times.

By this time, Clint was covered with slimy mud. He did not once complain or pause until the last cow was safely on shore. Then he walked slowly toward the wagon, breathing heavily, and she realized how tired he must be. He found a small stick and began to scrape what mud he could from his clothes. She rode over and could not help smiling at the sight he made.

"You sure didn't improve your appearance," she said, a twinkle in her eyes. "I've seen snapping turtles come out of that lake looking better."

Clint grinned and said nothing as the other riders now joined them. The three men who had been roping swung down and loosened the saddles on their almost exhausted mounts.

"Clint," Becky spoke with a note of pride in her voice. "I'd like you to meet my brother, Harvey. Harvey, this is Clint Austin, who's been staying at the ranch a few days."

Clint turned to meet the tall man who had been riding the flashy pinto horse. Harvey Major was several inches taller than Clint. He was a handsome man with black hair and mustache. His dark brown eyes held a smile as he extended his hand. His grip was strong and as Clint's eyes met Harvey's, they also caught for the first time the sparkle of the badge on the man's vest.

"Glad to meet you, Clint. We're in your debt for the help."

"Just glad I was around," responded the cowboy.

"This is my deputy Clyde Sykes," Harvey Major introduced the other rider. "Lucky we could get away for a while this morning. We'll have to be heading back soon. I have to testify at a trial in Santa Fe in a couple of days so I've got to go."

Clint shook hands with the deputy and then turned back to scrape a little more mud from his clothing. There was not much more he could do for the time being. He flipped the stick away and went to his horse. He mounted and waited for the others to tighten their cinches and swing back in their saddles. They spread out and began pushing the cattle away from the lake. At one point, Clint came close to Becky and he let his horse fall in beside hers. They were far enough from the others that his words would not carry to them.

"Sorry I grabbed you down by the lake," he apologized. He already knew enough of this woman to know she would resent any man touching her, even accidentally.

"I'm sure it was unintended." Her reply was cold and stiff and she turned her horse to trot away from him.

She was half angry at herself for the way she had spoken, since she knew Clint had done the only thing he could.

Clint understood the woman and it made him admire her all the more. He let his gaze follow her as she rode away from him. No doubt Becky's graceful figure had sent many a cowpuncher's mind into a whirl of wishful thoughts. Such a woman was not for the ordinary, drifting cowhand, that was for sure. However, you couldn't blame a man for looking . . . or for remembering what he saw.

Harvey and his deputy left them soon after they had the cattle strung out from the lake. The sheriff hated to leave. He gave Clint a friendly wave of his hand as he rode past the man riding drag.

"Stay as long as you can," he called to Clint. "They sure need the help . . . and, thanks."

Clint smiled and returned the wave and then watched the two men ride toward the wagon that was following the herd some distance back.

The day wore on. Now the cattle were no longer hunting water but spreading out to graze. They were much harder to drive than before they had reached the lake. When the cattle had strung out, Monte pulled the riders back to the wagon. They dismounted and loosened their cinches while Frank unpacked the lunch Helen had prepared. The sandwiches tasted good to the men who had had no breakfast and it was long past noon. The basket of fried chicken disappeared in minutes.

The wagon held several of the weaker calves, which bawled lustily as the riders ate their lunch nearby.

Becky and Clint worked the drag most of the afternoon. It was slow, hard work to keep the stragglers moving. Due to the late start and the delay at the lake, it would be long past dark before they reached the Major's drift fence and could turn the cattle loose. This part of the Major range was only fifteen miles from town but it was a long way to drive cattle, some with small calves. Besides, the cattle were new to the country and did not have any idea where they were going, which made it harder.

Dusk came and then twilight; they continued to push on. The moon rose and shed its pale light over the prairie, which let them see the cattle well enough to keep them moving and to distinguish some of the individual animals. Monte had now dropped back to help them at the rear of the herd.

"I've been missing a big, mottle-faced cow for about fifteen or twenty minutes," Becky told the old cowboy sometime after it had become fully dark. "She has been hanging back here all afternoon and now she is not around."

"Don't guess I've noticed her since I came back," Monte said. Becky was hand enough to notice a thing like this. "You sure she hasn't worked up ahead?"

"I'll bet not." The riders stopped their horses and a few minutes later Clint rode over to see what caused the delay. "Have you noticed the mottle-faced cow with the light-colored calf lately, Clint?" Becky asked.

The cowboy thought a moment. He knew the cow she meant, because they had been forcing her along all afternoon.

"The last time I remember seeing her was just before we crossed that little cedar draw about a quarter mile back."

"I don't think I've seen her since then, either," Becky said, twisting in her saddle to listen to the sound of the team and wagon following them.

Clint now turned and loped his horse up the right side of the herd for some ways and came slowly back, watching the cattle as they passed in front of him. He worked around the tail end of the herd and up the other side before he rode back to where the two riders sat on their horses.

"I don't think she's here," he stated flatly.

"I'll bet she got into those cedars," Becky said with a sigh. "It's a sure thing she didn't pep that calf up enough to take him up in the lead."

"Some of them could have slipped into those trees as dark as it is," Clint mused. "I sure don't think I've seen her since."

"I guess we can come back in the morning and see," Monte said in a tired voice. He began to turn his horse to follow the herd when he saw the girl shake her head.

"You two go on with the herd," Becky told them. "You both have done a lot more today than I have. I'll go back and see if I can locate them in that draw. There may be a bunch of them and by morning they could be scattered."

For a moment, Clint sat looking from the girl to the old cowboy, and it was a look of sheer wonderment. A man would ride a long ways and never find a pair like these two. The woman was already riding away.

"I'd better go with her, Monte," Clint drawled with a heavy sigh. "I once worked for a man who would horsewhip a fellow if he even thought a man would let a woman go back after those cows alone."

"Twenty years ago I'd have gone with her, too," grunted the white-haired cowboy. "She's as tired as any of us, which right now is right-smart tired."

Clint trotted his horse and caught up with Becky, drawing his horse up to walk beside her. Neither spoke. At the cedar draw they found more than fifteen cows and several calves scattered among the trees. It took them some time to force the cattle away from the trees and back on the trail. They worked in silence except to shout at the cattle, both too tired to think of anything to say. Becky did appreciate the cowboy coming back to help her. Not many men with regular jobs would put in the day this drifting stranger had put in for them. Again, it seemed he fit right in with the Major outfit.

Eventually, they came to the gate in the drift fence. It was open and they pushed the cattle through and were on Major range. Clint eased himself from his horse to close the gate. As he was fastening the top wire, he heard a horse loping toward them, and a moment later Monte's clear, high voice floated over the still air.

"Leave those dang cows and come on!" he called. "The others are scattered and the boys have long since headed for home. We got the calves out of the wagon and I sure hope their mammies find them before morning. Most of those little devils are as hungry as I am."

There was a light at the ranch when they reached it. Juan and Bud were in the kitchen waiting for the fire to get hot enough to make coffee. Becky went to help them get some food started while Clint and Monte took care of the horses. Frank was still at the barn unharnessing the team.

"I thought I'd worked for a tough outfit a time or two in my young life," Clint observed as he hung up his saddle. "But, by golly, I think this one takes all the prize money. Even the women on this outfit can ride you right into the ground."

"That Becky can outride most any man I ever knew," Monte grunted. "Her dad would be proud of her."

Clint smiled in the darkness. Becky wasn't the only one he admired. Old Monte was as tough as they came—too tough and too proud to ever admit the aches in his bones that night.

CHAPTER 7

FRANK Carlson went to town the next morning and returned the following day with his wife. Helen helped with the cooking so Becky could spend her full time with the ranch work. Vance's two children also came to the ranch, their schooling through for the year.

Frank stayed to help a few days, and on Saturday Harvey and his deputy Clyde Sykes came out to help but most of the work was done by the four men and Becky. Susan, ten, and Little Harvey, almost twelve, were constantly around the corrals and chutes. Aside from supervising their work at the corrals, Becky had turned over the care of the children to her sister.

Each morning, Clint told himself he should leave but the thought of Becky Major trying to handle the stock with such a short crew would not allow him to go. As it was, Becky did most of the actual branding while Clint and Bud worked the chute. Monte and Juan did the horseback work, with the help of the two youngsters. Clint again observed Juan Martinez— an excellent cowboy, a fearless rider, and among the best trainers of young horses he had ever worked around. The man never shirked his work and Clint was drawn to the likable, friendly rider. His feelings for Bud did not change. He had no respect for the big man, who did only what he had to and then reluctantly.

Finally, they ran the last steer through the chute and the branding of the grown stock was finished. The next morning they started on the calves. Juan roped and dragged them to the fire where Bud and Clint flanked and held them. Becky did the branding and Monte did the ear marking and castrating. Clint drove himself to do all he could. They were all tired and he had been amazed Becky had been able to stand up under the work as she had.

His admiration had grown each day for this woman. He liked her appearance, but her spirit and determination especially appealed to him. He tried to be near her as much as he could but even when near her he remained silent and reserved. While Becky appreciated all the man was doing, she couldn't help but wonder what his feelings toward her were. He was more than a help. He seemed to like to be near her but he said little and never let his feelings show beyond an occasional smile and a twinkle in his keen blue eyes.

They had been so busy with the branding that they had had no time to check their range for strays from the neighbors. Becky was greatly concerned some of the neighbors would have taken advantage of their inability to patrol the range and would be moving in on their pastures. The morning after they finished branding, she sent Bud and Juan to check on their new stock while the other three rode to check the Big Spring pasture—the nearest watering hole to the Payne and Cameron places. She was expecting to find stray stock. For the first time since Clint had been there, she wore the pearl-handled .38 Smith and Wesson pistol her brothers had given her years ago. From the way she wore the gun, Clint guessed the woman probably knew how to use it. Becky did not like carrying a gun, but she now knew their neighbors were not going to hold their cattle back unless forced to. Monte again offered to lend Clint a pistol but the cowboy smiled and refused. He did, however, put his rifle back on his saddle.

They did not have to look long to find the trouble Becky had anticipated. There were hundreds of cattle grazing near the Big Spring. From the sign, these cattle had been scattered there for well over a week. Some carried Payne or Cameron's brand and not a few belonged to the Farr ranch. There were even a few brands Monte did not recognize. Luckily none of their new cattle had drifted this far so they would not have to cut any out before they pushed out the strays.

Becky and Monte had started to gather the cattle, when Clint asked if he could ride to the top of the bluff where they had met Hal Flack the other time. He felt the bluff would be an ideal place to have someone watching to see if they moved the stock. Becky agreed quickly and he rode across the draw and up the winding trail to the top. He had ridden only a short distance across the flat country when he saw several riders coming up out of a draw. They rode directly toward him and he recognized the same five men he had met there the last time. He stopped his horse and drew the Winchester from the saddle boot, levered a shell into the chamber, and laid the rifle, fully cocked, across his left arm. The men watched as they slowly walked their horses toward him. They drew up about twenty feet from him in a rough semicircle.

"Well, if it ain't our Arizona-bound friend," the tall Farr foreman said, a thin smile sliding across his ruggedly handsome face. "I thought you was leaving the country for your health."

"You push too hard, Flack," Clint chided him mildly. "I guess I'm just a weak-willed individual. I couldn't stand your pressure and decided to stay until the Majors got their cattle settled."

Flack's smile grew into a broad grin. He had to admire the sandy-haired man's nerve. The foreman could read no fear in the man's blue eyes. Flack had not missed the fully cocked rifle or the confident manner in which it was held.

"Of course, I still intend to leave shortly, if I'm not pushed anymore. I'd leave quicker if some of you good neighbors was to quit trying to push in on Major grass," Clint observed.

"It is good grass this year," Flack said blandly, as though talking to an old friend. "Best I've seen here in years."

"Too bad it ain't yours," drawled Clint.

"Too bad the Majors don't own it either," Russ Payne

observed. His squinty eyes looked from under the extra-large black hat but they would not meet Clint's.

"Ain't that the truth," the tall, thin Sid Cameron agreed. "We need grass as much as they do."

"Well, I understand they do own that spring down there and they have controlled this grass for years," Clint drawled.

"That was when the old man was alive and the two boys were young fire eaters," Cameron admitted. "Becky Major may be a lot prettier than any of the others but she can't do what they did."

"She sure aims to try," Clint said bluntly.

"Boy, we sure are scared of that woman," Russ Payne mocked and spat around the large wad of tobacco he always chewed.

"You don't look very bright, either," Clint told him.

The long-faced Watson had been watching not only the cowboy before them but also the movement of the cattle in the basin below. He guessed Clint was merely trying to delay them until the others could gather the cattle and start them off Major grass.

"Somebody's moving our cows, Flack," the gunman said, pointing lazily to where Becky and Monte could be seen driving the cattle away from the water hole.

"Well, let's get down there and see if we can't talk a little better judgment into them," the foreman said. He waved his hand carelessly to Austin. "See you around . . . if you're fool enough to stay. . . . We're not going to play much longer."

"Neither am I." Clint nodded his head and reined his horse to watch them move carefully around him. Watson eyed him intently as he rode past, as though hoping for a chance. Clint gave him none.

They rode to the trail he had come up and dropped over the edge. As the last man went out of sight, he levered the shell out of the Winchester and rammed the rifle into the boot. He spurred his horse toward another part of the rim where he had observed the bank broke away a little less abruptly. He did not bother about trails but put his horse straight down the sloping side of the bluff.

It was a reckless thing to do, for the horse had to fight to keep his footing as he slid down the shale hillside. Clint reached the floor of the basin while the Farr riders were still twisting down the steep part of the trail.

Becky turned to see Clint loping toward her. As he approached, he took his rope down and began using it as a whip on the slower cattle. Soon the animals were running, driven by his rope and yells. She and Monte followed his example, and by the time Hal Flack reached the bottom of the bluff he could see only a cloud of dust as the cattle were stampeded away from them.

The men put their horses to a run to try to overtake their stock. At length, they caught up with the slowest cattle and the three riders driving them.

Becky looked over her shoulder to see Emil Watson drawing up behind her. She did not realize what he was going to do until he forced his horse close beside hers and reached down to catch her bridle rein. The man jerked her horse to a rough stop as she fought to regain control of her mount. She swung her fist at the man but missed. She fought desperately, trying to free the rein from the man's hand but he was too strong for her. Both failed to see Clint riding toward them at full speed, his rope doubled in his hand. Clint rode close and swung the doubled rope at Watson's head with all his strength. The long-faced rider took a terrific blow of the hard-twisted lariat across the side of his head and face. His hat flew off and he fell from his saddle without knowing what had hit him. The doubled lariat was almost as deadly as an iron bar.

Becky jerked the bridle rein from the falling man's hand and whirled her horse to follow the cowboy toward the knot of milling horses and men some distance away. Dust boiled up around them.

"They've got Monte!" she shouted.

Clint had also read the meaning of the dust and spurred his horse toward it. Monte had been pulled from his horse and was violently struggling between two men while Hal Flack tried to pin the old man's hands behind his back. The fourth man, still mounted, was holding the others' horses.

Clint pulled ahead of Becky and she watched as the cowboy charged the mounted man. She saw the doubled rope rise and strike again. A moment later, four horses with empty saddles loped off across the prairie. A man lay still among the sage where he had fallen.

Clint pulled his horse in a tight circle and charged the men on the ground, his rope ready. Hal Flack tried to use Monte as a shield, but the old man fought until he broke loose in time to dive out of the way as the lunging horse struck Flack with its shoulder. The foreman went sprawling in the sage as the rope swung out and ended in a dull whack across the head of red hair belonging to Sid Cameron. Again, the horse reared and whirled and Clint was charging the one man remaining on his feet. This man chose to run, ducking and turning in the sage and cactus. Russ Payne's big black hat protected his head some from the swinging rope. He managed to draw his pistol and get off one shot before the gun was knocked from his hand. He took an unmerciful beating until he finally fell whimpering in the dirt.

"Get up and walk back to the others," Clint commanded, his chest heaving.

Payne slowly got to his feet and stumbled forward, holding both hands to his throbbing head. Clint came close behind him on a very nervous horse, swinging the rope easily.

Becky watched them approach just as the Farr foreman was sitting up. From the corner of her eye she saw the man's hand move toward his pistol. Quickly, she drew the .38 and sent a bullet into the ground a few inches from the man's knee.

"Drop it, Flack!" The woman's voice was steady.

The man looked up to see the muzzle of the pistol was

now pointed at the center of his chest and did not waver. Even as she realized she had actually pointed a gun at a man, she read the surprise in his eyes and thought he had better believe where her next shot would go. A moment later, Monte kicked the gun from his hand and he felt his wrist go numb. He tried to get to his feet but one leg buckled under him and he fell back. He had not realized until then he had been hurt when the horse struck him.

"Take their guns, Monte," Becky said, her voice now tight.

"Harvey should never have given them back the other time," the old man said and snorted in disgust.

Sid Cameron's eyes had begun to focus again. He could see his hat several feet away, but it took some time for him to get his muscles coordinated to where he could reach for it. At last, his hand managed to pull it toward him. He put the hat on, still lying flat on the ground. It was several more minutes before he heaved his body to a sitting position and then stood up. He looked stupidly at the foreman still sitting on the ground rubbing his knee.

Monte mounted his horse and rode to where Watson lay unconscious. The old cowboy dismounted to remove the man's pistol, remounted, and loped back to the others.

"Let's just leave them here and go back to pushing those cows!" he shouted. "They can get home the best way they can."

"I think Doug's nose is broken," Sid Cameron said, bending over the man who had been holding their horses.

"I don't care if his whole head is caved in," Monte told him bluntly. "This should teach you never to lay a hand on Miss Major . . . and keep your damn cows off our grass!"

Much against Monte's wishes, Becky had them wait until all the men could stand up and walk under their own power. The man called Doug had a badly swollen nose and was unable to see out of his left eye. Watson had a rope burn across the side of his head he would carry to the day he died.

Hal Flack could barely walk. This would be a day none of them could ever forget.

Flack shook his head as the three Major riders loped off in the direction they had last seen the cattle. Twice now he had underestimated the fury and nerve of the sandy-haired cowboy.

"He'll pay for this," Watson promised grimly. "I'll force him to put on a gun so I can kill him."

Flack spoke bitterly. "So far, that boy's been at least two jumps ahead of us. He might just beat you with a gun, too, Emil."

"Not a chance," Watson boasted. "You've just lost your confidence."

"You may be right." Flack's knee almost buckled with each step he took. "But, I'm glad it will be you going up against him in a fight with a pistol, not me. I've got a hunch he just might know how to use one. I never dreamed a man could do the damage he did with just a lariat rope. Hell, if he had used a gun on us we would all be dead."

"Now I know how all them cows have felt that I've been beating with my rope all these years," Doug said bitterly. "I'm not sure I can ever see anything out of this eye."

A little later, the Major riders caught the riderless horses. Knowing Hal Flack's knee was badly hurt, Clint tied the foreman's horse to a tall sage. The others had their reins tied to the saddle horns and were driven ahead of the riders along with the cattle.

They forced the cattle to stay at a run until their mounts gave out with exhaustion. They rested a short time but as soon as the horses had gotten their second wind, they ran the cattle some more. It certainly did not do the stock any good to be treated this way. However, Monte was not satisfied until they had passed across Payne's ranch and scattered the cattle in the low cedar-covered hills beyond his usual territory.

"Why don't we push the next bunch to the east, rather

than drive them right back to their home territory?" Becky asked as they turned their horses toward home.

"We haven't had any neighbors pushing us except from the west. If we push these cows off on the neighbors to the east, they would push back and we would be in more trouble than we are now," Monte answered. "However, we could push the next bunch into the badlands to the northwest. It would take longer to find them and push them back in on us."

"Well, you had better make it as rough on them as you can," Clint drawled, his voice carrying a grim tone. "They don't aim to quit pushing you."

"You sure made yourself some real enemies today," Monte growled and urged his horse to a trot. The tired animal responded sluggishly. "At least that Waston fellow will be gunning for you after this. I'd feel better about it if you'd put on a pistol."

For a second, the inner man flashed in Clint's blue eyes but he said, "I've managed up to now."

"Well, I've got to admit you've done that," Monte said, smiling dryly. "I just ain't sure your luck can hold out forever."

"It can't." They noticed for the first time a note of pessimism in the cowboy's tone. "If I stay after this it can only lead to trouble. Flack isn't going to let anyone do what I've been doing to him. I've already stayed much longer than I intended. I don't want Flack to think I'm running, so I'll ride a few more days. Then, I've just got to pull out."

Becky watched the man's face as he spoke—more than he had in days. She could not help but wonder why the man felt he had to go. Surely he wasn't running from anything. Yet, he seemed so reluctant and torn between staying and leaving. If he was running from something, what? But she had to admit he had no reason to stay. Their fight was nothing to him—he had already done more to help them than was called for from a close friend, let alone a man just riding through. Still, how would they cope with Hal Flack without him? So far, at each encounter, Clint was what had made the difference. Without him, they would already have been whipped.

CHAPTER 8

SEVERAL days passed without further incident, and Becky began to hope this meant their neighbors had decided the Major grass was not worth another fight. Peace did not last long, however. Juan found several hundred strays that had been pushed in on their range during the night. Their own cattle were now scattered over the range, and it took them long hours of hard riding to separate the strays and drive them beyond their border. They pushed two bunches into the badlands.

As soon as one bunch was driven off, another was pushed in from a different direction. They saw no riders, as each bunch was now driven in after dark. Becky's small crew rode from daylight to dark trying to clear their pastures. It was hopeless. Yet, they tried. If they did not drive the strays back, there would not be enough grass for the Major stock. The constant working of their own cattle made the animals wild and restless and kept them from putting on weight.

Frank Carlson brought the first good news they had heard in a long time. The cattle market had suddenly gone sky high. The cattle they had purchased a few months before were now worth considerably more, possibly twice as much, even in their thin condition. Everyone in the territory was elated over the great improvement in the market. In celebration, Fisher was going to throw a big party in Sundown the next Saturday night.

On Friday, Frank returned to the ranch with supplies and the additional news that Vance was to return from Ojo Caliente—his foot was finally beginning to heal. This was all

Becky needed to make up her mind. They would go into town for the party.

Becky left Saturday morning with the Carlsons and the two children in the spring wagon. They were hardly out of sight when the men began taking turns at their baths in the round tub in the bunkhouse. All except Clint. The tall, thin rider lay on his bed with his legs crossed and his arms folded behind his head. It was sure a good feeling not to have to do anything but rest. Occasionally, he dozed off for a few minutes, his mouth slacking open, a little snore pushing forth. Bud and Juan finished their preparations and went to the corrals for their horses but Monte stayed to speak to Clint.

"Sure you ain't comin'?" he asked and sat on the bed beside the man. Clint brought himself back from a doze to look sleepily at the white-haired man above him. "There'll be lots of pretty girls there," Monte assured him.

"I doubt that would do me much good." Clint managed a sleepy grin. "I'd never have a chance at any woman with you around."

"True, true." Monte turned to look out through the door at the summer sunshine. "Could be some excitement."

"You planning to steal somebody's wife?" the cowboy asked blandly. "Why, you're much too young to marry."

"Ah, go on," Monte snorted, giving the man an affectionate shove. "I could have been married eight, ten times by the time I was your age."

"Women were much easier to find in those bygone days. Right?"

"Oh, hell no. The men were just better looking."

"Boy, you sure couldn't prove that by anything I've seen." Clint now turned serious. "I don't think it would be smart for me to go, Monte. I would sure run into Flack or Watson. I'm planning on leaving, anyway. I can't see any point in asking for more trouble."

"You're probably right." Monte sighed heavily and stood

up. "I guess I'd do the same. You've sure done more than enough." He walked to the door and stopped to look back at the man on the bed. "I'd feel better though if you was there to back me if Vance tries to tangle with them. They will respect you—after what you've done to them, they can't help but worry about what you might do next. When Becky tells Vance what's been going on, he is sure to try to take them all on, bad leg or no."

Clint really did not want to go. However, a bond of friendship had formed between himself and this white-haired cowboy. He knew Monte would do his best for his outfit no matter what the odds. Clint respected this attitude so much he could not do less. The outfit you rode for came first in his order of things. Always had.

He rolled off the bunk and walked to the washstand. "You rattle on like an old woman," he said as he poured water into the tub.

"That's a lot better than being a wooden Injun like some people," Monte teased. "I'll go down and saddle our horses." As he stepped away from the door a smile of relief crossed beneath the white mustache.

The two Major riders arrived in town in time to buy a few items at the store and get their hair cut before drifting out to the party at the Fisher residence at the edge of town.

Charles Fisher was the most prosperous businessman in the county. Last year, he had been elected to the state legislature. Much of his wealth had come from the cattlemen, and he often gave a party for them and their riders in appreciation of their patronage. This year, the celebration was extra large. After all, hadn't the cattle market been pushing to a record high? Why, some of his customers might even pay off all they owed him.

Long tables had been set under the big, spreading cottonwood trees at the Fisher home, which surrounded a large, spacious lawn. Monte and Clint followed through the line at the tables and received heaping plates of beef, pork, salad, vegetables, and other good things to eat. They found a spot under one of the big trees at the far end of the yard to sit down. Clint's eyes searched the crowd for the faces of the Farr riders. He saw Russ Payne with his wife but the squat rancher never seemed to glance his way.

From where they sat cross-legged on the grass, Clint watched a young man in expensive town clothes escort Becky through the serving line. Tonight, Becky did not resemble the tomboy from the ranch who could work cattle as many hours as any hand on her crew. Her hair shone wavy honey gold in the light of the big lanterns, and the dark green dress she wore set off her deep brown eyes like two sparkling jewels in her suntanned face. Long sleeves hid the marked differ-ence between the white of her arms and the brown of her hands. There was no denying she was a very attractive woman. Clint asked Monte who the young man was.

"Tim Harding. He's a real home guard," the old cowman grunted. "Not really a bad fellow, just a home guard. His dad owns a big outfit forty miles south of here. Real big spread and old Flint Harding is a real old-time cowman, like old man Major. Real tough old man."

The sight of the beautiful young woman next to the handsome man in his expensive suit made Clint feel conspic-uous in his range garb. True, there were many there in the same but it made him feel out of place as far as Becky was concerned. He knew that no drifting cowboy would ever win that woman's hand, and his spirits sank to a new low. Again, he told himself to ride on out of this. Well, he should be able to leave with his head high after tonight. He would leave in the morning.

The meal was finished and servants came to remove the dishes and take down the tables. A group of musicians took their positions near the house and began to play, and soon couples were dancing on the even carpet of green lawn. Frank Carlson and Vance Major now joined the two riders at the far end of the grass. When Monte introduced Vance to

Clint, Vance awkwardly reached past his crutch to shake the cowboy's hand. Vance had the same brown eyes Becky and Harvey had, but he was neither as handsome nor as tall as the sheriff. Clint could tell the man felt the crutches made him appear weak.

Vance asked Monte about the ranch and Clint listened as the old cowboy deliberately tried to put a bright side on his reply. The old man went out of his way to brag on the way Becky was handling things. Clint wondered what Becky had already told Vance and if he realized Monte was trying to cover up just how bad things were.

The dancing was under way when the Carl Farrs and the Harvey Majors arrived. Farr's steel gray hair flashed brightly in the lamplight as the man smiled broadly to people who called and waved. His trim wife also acknowledged the greetings. She had a warm and friendly way about her, which was truly reflected in the greetings she received. The greetings to her husband were more from admiration and respect and he beamed with his pride. He knew he was the big man in this community.

Beth Major was a tall, strikingly pretty blonde woman, and anyone could tell the sheriff was extremely proud of his wife. When Clint mentioned this to Monte, he was surprised to learn Mrs. Harvey Major was the only daughter of the Carl Farrs. No wonder the sheriff did not push the Farrs.

Their host now came running to make these important folks feel especially welcome and took them into the house for a special serving of the dinner.

A few moments later, several faces shone with open surprise at the appearance of another couple. Smokey Bennett and his mousy-looking little wife emerged shyly from the group near the musicians. Sarah Bennett's frightened little eyes flitted from face to face, never stopping for more than an instant on anyone. She did not feel at home here. Most of the people understood why. Her husband had just returned from serving time in the state prison, having been sent there for stealing cattle. Harvey Major had been responsible for sending him there.

Smokey, however, laughed and beamed at folks and seemed to thoroughly enjoy himself. The short man's dark hair was slicked down and shown in the lamplight. His sunburned face was ruggedly good looking and he joked with anyone who spoke to him.

The evening progressed and more people joined the dancers. Clint noticed many of the men would make short trips to a certain door at the rear of the house. When they returned, their faces glowed a little more and their enjoyment of the dance seemed greater. Clint suggested they take a little walk and investigate this door and the others readily agreed. Of course, all except Clint already knew what they would find there. They walked along the outside of the lawn so as not to interfere with the dancers who were now having a lively square dance. They walked slowly so Vance could easily keep up. Clint let his eyes go to the girl in the dark green dress. She had danced every dance so far and the cowboy thought some of those town folks would be wondering how she could dance so long without resting. Well, he knew. If any cowboy there thought he could dance the legs off Becky, he had another think coming. Clint smiled to himself at this thought and a tingle of pride went through him. He realized his place but he still greatly admired that woman. Behind the door inside a large room a group of men gathered around a keg of whiskey, which awaited one and all. Since some of the people who attended these affairs frowned on drinking, Fisher would never serve whiskey at the tables, but all the natives knew that a keg of good drinking whiskey would be somewhere on the premises.

The room was quite full as Monte swung the door wide so Vance could enter. Several of the men who looked up to see the Major group entering carried bruises and burns from Clint's rope. Doug had a large bandage covering his left eye. As Clint entered, they eyed him sullenly. He was man enough to meet their eyes and his own keen blue ones flashed a plain warning to each man. Watson's long face was full of pure hate for him. Had they been anywhere else, the man would have challenged Clint then and there.

Shortly after the Major group had passed through the doorway, Carl Farr excused himself from his wife and started in the direction of that same door.

"Don't stay too long, Carl," his wife called after him. "I came here to dance, not visit."

The big man turned to smile kindly at her but his eyes told her to mind her own business. He turned away again and she turned her attention back to the ladies around her as Harvey Major stood up to follow Farr. Beth looked at her husband's departing back and smiled. She made no attempt to stop him.

The Major group had hardly had time to fill their cups and find places to stand when Farr and Harvey came in. Russ Payne worked his ever-present chaw of tobacco around his mouth as he hurriedly got to his feet to get a clean cup for the important man. Quickly, he filled it and gave it and his chair to Farr. As he watched, Vance Major smiled thinly, while old Monte snorted in his cup. Farr turned to look sharply at the old cowboy. Monte's eyes met Farr's squarely, with neither respect nor fear. They plainly said, too hell with you, big man. While others openly showed embarrassment at the old cowman, Farr smiled broadly and turned his attention to his cup. Inwardly, he was boiling at the open insult. Damn that old man—there had to be a way to break him.

"Sure is a nice night for a party, ain't it, Mr. Farr?" a man asked trying to relieve the tension that had come over the room.

"Fine night." Farr tasted the whiskey. "Fine whiskey, too."

"The cow market sure has gone up," another man said.

"Cattle's worth more today than they ever was," observed another.

"For sure they're worth a lot more than they was a few

SADDLE A WHIRLWIND ■ 97

months ago," Russ Payne added. He took another long drink from his cup. "In fact, they're darn near worth twice what they was a year ago. By the way, Mr. Farr, are you shipping any of your cattle at these high prices?"

"No, not yet, Russ. I think they will go higher."

Clint guessed several men in the room would now delay selling the cattle they had planned to sell immediately, just from that one remark of the big man. Vance smiled and Monte again snorted in his cup as Farr's face colored slightly.

Two more men entered the room. At sight of them, Vance's dark eyes flashed. Hal Flack and Sid Cameron stood silently by the door, their eyes going over the room.

"Well, I see you two can still locate a keg of whiskey," Vance told them in his short, abrupt way. "It's too bad you can't locate your cows and keep them on your own grass."

"My cows been bothering you, too, Vance?" Russ Payne spoke from the front of the room. A sneer pushed across his tobacco-stained face. He wanted to show Mr. Farr he was not afraid of the Majors.

"You ain't got the guts to do it on your own, Russ," Vance said without looking at the little man. "I think Flack and Sid have been teaching you bad habits."

Flack met Vance's eyes blandly but Cameron would look only toward the floor. A dark rope burn ran the length of his left cheek.

"Maybe all of you thought because I wasn't there you could push your stock on Major grass. Well, I'm telling all of you right here and to your face that you had better keep your cows off our grass!" Vance let his eyes challenge each man.

"You threatenin' me, Vance? What did you say about me not having any guts?" Payne bristled and stepped around the group to take several steps toward the man on crutches. His eyes met Clint Austin's and he stopped short.

"Hold on, now!" Harvey Major interposed smoothly. "Vance ain't threatening anyone . . . warning, maybe."

The tall Farr foreman seemed only amused at what was

going on. Clint could read the self-assuredness behind the expression in the hawklike eyes. It did not matter what Vance Major, or anyone else said. Hal Flack worked for the big man, Carl Farr, and he would do whatever Farr told him to do. Russ Payne looked across the room as if wanting Flack to signal what to do next. The foreman lifted his eyebrows ever so slightly. Sid Cameron looked sick.

"Look, Vance," Payne now called heatedly. "When you Majors was big enough to hold all that grass, it was yours. You just don't walk that big anymore."

"Apparently my outfit was big enough to throw you off our grass the last time they caught you. In fact, from the looks of several of you, I'd think you'd remember not to come back. I hope you had a nice walk home." Vance spoke savagely, and Clint knew Becky had told her brother of their last incident. "Since you don't seem to remember too well, I'll step outside with you, Russ."

"I'll not fight a cripple," Payne taunted, watching the hurt pride come into Vance's eyes.

"*I'm* no cripple," Harvey Major snapped. "You'll fight me in a minute, if you keep this up. What Vance says goes for all of us Majors. You boys keep your cows off our range."

"Now hold on, boys," Carl Farr interjected. "Let's not have any arguments here. After all, we're all guests, remember?" Farr got up and refilled his cup from the keg. As he continued, he was amused at the surprised look his words brought to several faces in the room. "You see, Vance, I admit I may be somewhat to blame for your trouble. You weren't going to need all your range this spring, as you had no stock. I knew that, as did most of the men in this room. I felt you were under some obligation to me, so I told my foreman to put some of our stock on your grass. Perhaps some of the others got the idea your range was opened up to anyone."

"Well, by God, it ain't!" Vance snapped.

"Well, you *will* admit you're under some obligation to me?"

A smirk came over Farr's lips as he spoke. "Surely you don't mind me using a little grass in return for my favors to you."

"I let no man push his cattle on my land without getting permission . . . first. No man! Not even you, Mr. Farr!" Vance was adamant in his statement, but after a short pause he met his defeat, knowing without the loan from Farr he could not have restocked his range. "If you were to make arrangements in advance, we might have had to let you use a little grass . . . only because we are obligated to you. We aren't obligated to any of these others."

"Now, I'll remember that," Carl Farr spoke evenly, relishing his victory. Then he added softly, "Who shall I ask? You've been away. Your brother says he's not running the place."

Harvey Major spoke just as softly as his father-in-law. "Becky is running the ranch until Vance is able to come home. I have told you before. You might try asking her."

"Is that an order, Harvey?" Farr bristled.

"Only a suggestion, Daddy Farr." The sheriff's brown eyes met his father-in-law's squarely. He did not blink. "A suggestion you would be wise to follow. Becky is running the ranch but I'll sure back her if there is trouble. All of you had best remember that."

Sharp words formed on Carl Farr's tongue but his wisdom kept them from being said. After all, he had won his victory. Vance now hobbled from the room almost like a whipped dog.

Monte felt his heart sink. He knew Vance felt he was having to hide behind a big brother and a little sister. Nothing could be more humiliating to a man of Vance's nature. The memories of being the little boy at home were bitter in his mind. The old cowboy caught Clint's eye and the two put their cups on the table to quietly follow Vance. Once outside, they let Vance go his way, knowing he would want to be alone. The two cowboys walked around the dancers to the end of the lawn and sat down on the grass under a large lilac bush.

They had been there only a few minutes when Hal Flack made his way around the dancers limping at each step to come and squat down before them. He winced slightly as his weight rested briefly on one knee.

"I'm obliged to you for leaving the horse." The man's voice was soft as he looked from one man's face to the other. "I don't think I could have made it home on this leg."

"It sure as hell wasn't my idea," Monte assured him.

"Oh, I know that. I know whose idea it was and I appreciate it." He was silent a few moments, then gave them the message he had come for. Though he spoke to both of them, his words were for Clint only. "There's no use fighting a lost cause. You can't possibly hold out against the odds. If the Majors would just listen to reason, Mr. Farr would let me help you keep the others off that range. He don't want it all and you would still have some of it. That's a lot better than losing it all, even though it might hurt some folks' pride."

"You can tell Carl Farr we ain't going to give him one damn blade of that grass!" Monte exploded.

The foreman continued to speak calmly, as though he had not heard the old cowboy. "Becky Major can't hold that grass. Her brothers would have a great big job but I say it's impossible for a woman."

"She'll sure give it one hell of a try," Clint told him evenly. "She's no ordinary woman."

"That she ain't," agreed the foreman. "You've been lucky so far and I'll admit that, Austin. You've gotten the best of us twice. However, your luck has run out. Nobody ever took a gun from Watson, let alone twice. He's so mad about that he may shoot you whether you put on a gun or not. I feel I owe you one for leaving the horse so I'm trying to control him, but I don't know how much longer I can do it. Now, Mr. Farr and I admire your nerve but you're just on the wrong side. Listen to a little reason. We can all come out with some of what we want if we quit fighting each other."

"I don't run the outfit," Clint said, as though reminding

the man. "So I couldn't make them quit fighting you even if I wanted to."

"True, maybe, but you're the one who has kept us from doing what we want. Without you, my job would be over and we would have their grass."

"I'm not too sure of that. Becky Major don't give up. Anyway, I'm about ready to leave. The only thing keeping me is the thought of leaving Becky Major to the Farr vultures."

"Vultures may pick your bones. It might be better to leave and enjoy the rest of your years. I'll warn you again, I can't hold Emil Watson off forever."

"Let me warn you, too, Flack," Monte cut in as the foreman stood up to leave. "No Major ever gave up without a fight. Becky is as fine as any of them. She may be at a disadvantage, being a woman, but you'll not get an acre of grass from her!"

Flack shrugged his shoulders and flexed his leg as he stood up. He turned away and spoke over his shoulder. "One way or another, Monte."

Becky had watched Vance come from the room at the rear of the house and then disappear into the crowd. She had watched Monte and Clint as they talked to the Farr foreman by the lilac bush. She wondered what they could be saying. She could tell Monte was upset but the other two seemed to be speaking calmly.

She danced another dance with Tim Harding and then she danced one dance with the graceful Farr foreman. Hal Flack was a good dancer, although his knee was still bothering him. Hal's manner, when he chose, could be quite engaging and friendly.

Ever since first coming to this territory, Flack had admired this brown-eyed woman. He could not help feeling someday she would come to respect him. Sooner or later, she and her brothers would have to come to terms with his employer or be removed completely from their range. If she would just realize it, he could make things easier for her. The dance over, he thanked her politely and hurried away.

Several times during the evening Becky caught herself looking toward the thin cowboy sitting on the grass beside Monte. Clint had not seemed to take any interest in the dancing, for she had not seen him with any of the young ladies present. She could not help wondering if he knew how to dance or if he was ashamed to ask her to dance with him.

Tim Harding left her to get some punch, and for a brief moment she was alone. She felt someone come and stand beside her and a man's hand touched her lightly on the arm. Perhaps it was the memory of his touch on her leg that day at the lake that stirred her so. At any rate, she knew he was now going to ask her to dance, and it suddenly annoyed her that he had waited so long.

"Good evening, boss lady," the cowboy drawled in that slow, civil way he had.

"Good evening, yourself."

He began rather shyly. "I'm not known for my dancing ability but I'd sure like to have one dance with you in my memories."

For some unknown reason, a strong urge to tease him came over her. How would he take teasing? Of course, she would be glad to dance with him but she had never teased him before and her words came as a complete surprise to him.

"My father had one very strict rule about us girls," she said trying to make her voice sound serious. "He never allowed any of us to dance with one of the hired men."

She intended to say she would make an exception in his case but his look of utter astonishment and disbelief stopped her momentarily. His face grew crimson and his blue eyes held a look she would never forget. Without a word, he swung on his heel and walked swiftly away from her.

"Wait, Clint!" she called after him.

The man did not look back or slacken his stride. A moment later he disappeared in the darkness outside the light of the lanterns. Becky watched him go, sorry and very angry with herself. Why had she chosen that moment to tease him? Why did she even think she knew him well enough to do it?

Some time later Monte found Clint in the now almost deserted refreshment room, a cup in his hand. Neither spoke as the white-haired rider filled a cup for himself. Monte took a sip and watched Clint finish his drink. The thin rider spun the cup across the table and started toward the door.

"What's the rush, son? Plenty whiskey left."

"I've had more tonight than I've had in the past six years. See you in the morning."

"Goin' home?"

"For tonight. I'm leaving in the morning."

The door swung shut behind Clint and Monte knew better than to follow. He did not know what had happened but he knew Becky must have said something that had upset Clint as nothing else had done. In fact, until now, nothing seemed to upset Clint's even nature.

Monte slowly drank the whiskey, his mood no better for it. He lingered over his cup as other patrons drifted back to help empty the keg. The old cowboy took no part in their loud and boisterous talk, keeping strictly to himself. He thought, Flack was right—that quiet cowboy had been the only thing that stood in Farr's way. Monte knew Clint would leave now and he kept wondering how he would keep things going for his employer. Well, he'd been holding things together on the Major ranch for over twenty years. By God, he'd do it some way . . . but he would miss Clint. He felt he was losing a friend, even though he had not known the man long. He couldn't remember when he had felt so alone.

CHAPTER 9

THE party reached the midway point, and the musicians stopped to rest while the dancers lined up to partake of the many and varied refreshments their hosts provided. The tables were again brought from the house and filled with fancy cakes, pies, cookies, and candies. Carl Farr carried a plate filled with the good things to his wife and returned to the tables as though to get another for himself. However, he did not stop at the tables this time but drifted away from the crowd now gathering around the refreshments and disappeared into the darkness of the night. When he was certain he was neither watched nor followed, he made his way to the barn at the far end of the Fisher property. Here, he was soon joined by his foreman and big Bud Jarvis.

"Smokey coming?" he asked Flack.

"Russ is bringing him and Cameron."

"Good." The rancher turned to Bud. "Can't you keep the Majors off our backs, Bud? That's what I'm paying you to do."

"Not without getting shot. Monte has his eye on me and they keep that damn Mexican with me all the time. He'd tell them in a minute if he caught me helping you."

"Maybe you had better take care of him so he can't tell them anything," Farr suggested. "Do a better job than you did on Austin. Try and keep us informed as to what they're doing."

A few minutes later three men slipped into the complete darkness of the barn's long entryway. A match flared and Flack checked the faces, then quickly snuffed out the light.

"Thanks for coming, boys," Farr said softly.

"Let's get down to business," Smokey Bennett said and grunted. "I don't think much of meeting like this."

Farr spoke smoothly. "On the contrary, Smokey, this is a perfect place. Where else could we all get together with less excuse?"

"Have it your way, Mr. Farr. Just tell me what part I have in your plans."

"Well, my plans are going pretty well. Vance Major was really upset tonight."

"He better lay off me, if he knows what's good for him," Russ Payne boasted. "I've been waiting for a chance like this for years."

"It's really not Vance we have to worry about. How about this fellow Austin?" Farr asked.

"Aw, he's just been plain lucky so far. He took us by surprise. Watson will handle him next time."

"He's got a lot more than just luck," Flack said very softly. The foreman's voice held genuine respect. "Austin will fight and we know he can fight rough."

"One man can't stop us from using that grass!" Payne asserted, still boastfully.

"Well, he's sure managed to keep us from enjoying any of it up till now," the foreman observed coldly.

"I'll have to admit you're perfectly right, Hal," Farr agreed. He rubbed his thick hands together across his belted middle. "Why do you think he is staying on with the Majors? What's he getting out of it? They can't pay him that much."

"Maybe he thinks he'll get Becky Major," Russ suggested behind his snicker.

"He'd no doubt like that," Flack admitted ruefully. "So would I. No, Mr. Farr, I think he would have ridden on out if we hadn't tried to force him. He just won't be pushed."

"He's not very smart," Farr snapped. "We'd pay him two or three times what they can pay him."

"There are a few men who can't be bought, Mr. Farr," Flack drawled. "I don't think he's in it for the pay. I think he's one of those fellows who fights for what he believes in. You may not like him or agree with him but he has made them one great friend and us one hell of an enemy."

"You sound like you're on his side!"

"No, sir, but I do respect him." The foreman rubbed his chin in the darkness. "I guess I even envy him a little, as he is still trying to believe all the things I did when I was a kid."

"It's time you grew up!" Farr snapped, not liking this conversation in the least.

"Oh, I'm full-growed, Mr. Farr. I know what makes the world go 'round—money . . . land . . . power. We all want more. There ain't enough to go around so the strong take from the weak. I long ago learned who was the strong man around here. I went into this with my eyes wide open and I'll do my part, whatever it takes . . . but, I can't help but admire a man who don't have a price on his principles."

"Like you and me?"

"If you say so, Mr. Farr."

"How about you, Sid? You like the way things are going?" Farr asked, changing to a new opinion.

"Hell, no. My cattle are nothing but skin and bones because they've had the hell run out of them so many times." The tall rancher spoke with no enthusiasm. "To be honest, Mr. Farr, I don't like things at all. I thought we would move in on that grass and my cattle would get fat and sassy. I never dreamed a woman and a few riders could do what they have done. No, sir. I don't like it at all."

"I really don't care what you like, Sid. Do as you are told or find another banker!" Farr spoke testily now. "I've stalled on foreclosing on you only for your help in this!"

"This family quarrel is all well and good but just where do I come in?" Smokey Bennett asked. He had heard quite enough of this bickering.

"Well, the whole thing is, Smokey, I'm afraid I didn't take enough into consideration in my original plans. Take this fellow Austin, for example," Farr admitted, his tone altogether different when speaking to the little rustler. Now, his voice was cordial and friendly. "Now, I hold a mortgage on all the Majors' deeded land to secure the money I loaned them to buy cattle. I thought we could just keep pushing cows in on that grass and keep things kinda messed up for them, then they wouldn't be able to make any profit on those cows and would be forced to sell out to me. Vance being hurt played right into my hands."

"Instead, the cow market goes up like crazy and they could sell today and have money to pay off your note and still have a few cows left to start over with." Smokey Bennett was quick to catch what Farr meant.

"Right!"

"So, where do I come in?"

"Why, the thought came to me you might be interested in getting a little even with the Majors for the way Harvey forced you to take a few years' vacation, so to speak," Farr said mildly. From the snort the rustler gave, Farr knew he had not misjudged the man. "I thought so." He sighed with satisfaction. "Now, what I have in mind is for you to move a few of the Majors' cows."

"Steal them?" Smokey laughed softly. "No, thanks, Mr. Farr. Harvey Major may be your son-in-law but no one could keep him off my back the first time they missed a cow!"

"Did I mention stealing? I wasn't aware I had spoken that word. Why, the thought never entered my mind. I would have no part in anything illegal." Farr's tone was now like acid. "Why, I don't want you to ever steal another cow, Smokey. I mean that! My idea was for you to slip in and split off a bunch of their cows and scatter them in the badlands. You know that rough country better than anyone. Every chance you get, grab another bunch and scatter them far enough for it to take them a long time to find them. Even longer to get them back on their own grass."

"Oh, I get it. With me chasing their stuff off and you

pushing yours on, they can't possibly hold things together. Not with what riders they have."

"That's the idea, Smokey. I've seen to it they can't hire any more help. Austin slipped in on us from out of the county, but they won't find any more. If you hide their stock well enough, they won't find them in time to sell them to pay me. Hell, the market won't stay up forever."

"You've got a real smart thing there, Mr. Farr. I guess it's all legal, too," Bennett admitted ruefully. "However, I don't see what good it will do me, other than a little personal satisfaction. I'll admit it would be nice, but it ain't exactly what I need the most of now."

"I thought you could maybe use a little cash money, Smokey. You probably haven't been able to save much the last few years. Now, suppose you send me a bill for moving stock, say two bits a head for grown stuff. I'll take your count and pay you promptly when I receive your bill."

"All that besides getting back at Harvey Major," Hal Flack put in. "As long as you don't change a brand or try to sell a cow, they can't very well pin a rustlin' charge on you."

"It ain't a bad idea," Smokey mused. He now turned to the barn door and partly opened it to peer outside. "I could sure use the cash."

"Then you'll do it?" Farr asked.

"If you get a bill for cattle moving in the next few weeks . . . please pay promptly. I don't like to have to make collections," the short rustler spoke softly. "Now, I'm going to get out of here. I think I hear someone coming from the house."

"Damn, I think maybe there's some snooper down by the other end of the corral, too," Flack said. He had stepped to the door near the rustler and was peering out over the short man's shoulder.

"Russ, you go out and stall whoever it is coming from the house until we can slip out another way and get back to the party," Farr instructed in a loud whisper. "Bud, you crawl out that side window and see if there is someone snooping around the corrals."

"I'll bet it's that damn Mexican," muttered Bud.

"If it is, you take care of him and don't mess it up like you did with Austin," Flack instructed softly.

Russ Payne eased out the door and walked loudly along the path toward the house. He had reached the corner of the barn when he saw young Tim Harding approaching. Upon recognizing the man, Russ gave an inward sigh of relief. He knew he had nothing to fear from Harding.

"What the hell do you want?" Payne demanded angrily.

"Why, I'm looking for Clint Austin," the young man stammered, taken off guard by the other's belligerent manner. "He rides for the Majors."

"What do you want with him?"

"Miss Major wants him . . . not that it's any of your damn business," Tim snapped, resenting the man's questions. His attitude became both calm and cool. Payne had no reason to push him.

"Well, he sure ain't around here," Payne told him, tartly. "I've been down here checking the horses and there ain't no Major rider gonna put his horse in with mine."

Tim turned on his heel and stomped back toward the house. The rancher followed a few steps behind him.

Becky was sorry when Tim reported he could not find Clint. The cowboy must have returned to the ranch, and the apology she was determined to offer would have to wait.

When the party finally broke up, Tim drove her to her house where she would spend what little remained of the night. She dismissed Tim quickly at the door, thanking him for bringing her home, and went inside. Tim shook his head as he walked back to his buggy. While Becky had never permitted him to kiss her, she had never before dismissed him so abruptly.

Sarah Bennett was glad the ordeal was over at last. This had been the first time she had been at a public function since her husband's conviction. It had not been her idea to go tonight—Smokey had insisted and she did not know why. It had not seemed to bother him to be among the people who sent him to prison. It had been unnerving to her. She hoped he would not insist on attending another such function as long as she lived.

The Bennett ranch was in one of the larger canyons of the badlands. It was a long way from town, and daylight was breaking in the east when they reached the halfway point. Here, Smokey drew the buckboard to a halt.

"What's wrong?" she asked.

"Nothing." He turned to rummage behind the seat. "I need a little refreshment."

"Didn't you have enough at the party?" A tinge of fear crept into the woman's voice.

"Now, don't you go nagging me, Sarah," he warned.

He tipped the bottle back and drank heavily. As the buckboard moved ahead, the woman drew herself away from him as far as she could on the narrow seat. The balance of the ride was made in silence, just as many of them had been in years past. At regular intervals, Smokey tipped the bottle to his lips. It was a pattern all too familiar to her. At the house, events continued in their old ways. He let her unhook and unharness the team while he finished the bottle. When she had finished, he followed her on unsteady legs into the house. Once inside, he suddenly reached out to grasp her arms.

"Don't Smokey!" the woman screamed and twisted in an attempt to get away from him. "You promised you'd never beat me again if I waited for you!"

"I ain't too sure you waited!" he accused drunkenly.

"Oh, Smokey, you know better than that!" Her eyes pleaded with him from her white face. "Please don't hit me, please!"

"Cut out that naggin', woman!" he told her gruffly, pulling her toward him.

He kissed her roughly and then pushed her away to hold her at arm's length. Suddenly, he lashed out at her with a closed fist. The force of the blow sent her reeling back. She went over a chair and fell heavily. Instantly she scrambled to her feet, screaming, and managed to push the chair against him as he rushed for her. He had anticipated this move, however, and the chair only partly tripped him. As he fell, he managed to grab her around one ankle, dragging her to the floor with him.

Sarah screamed, kicked, and even bit his hand but it availed her nothing, for she could not match his brute strength. Slowly, he worked his way up her body until his weight held her helpless and his fists beat her into black unconsciousness.

When she came to sometime later he was asleep on the sofa, one foot draped ungracefully over the back. She managed to push herself to her feet and half drag herself to their room where she collapsed across the bed.

Clint was in his bed only a few hours that night and he slept but little of that. His mind had turned over and over the memory of Becky telling him he was not good enough to dance with her. How could he have been so fooled by her actions at the ranch? It was indeed a bitter hurt to have her speak to him as she had. Well, when morning came he would just saddle his horse and ride on. He had been a complete fool to have stayed and taken a hand in this fight, anyway. It was nothing to him whatever happened to the Majors.

Shortly after dawn he rolled over in his bed and looked over to see if Monte was awake. The white head appeared above the blankets, and the even breathing told him that the old man was still dead to the world. It had been a long hard night for Monte, too. Clint's eyes went to Bud's bed. The young giant was snoring softly.

Juan's bed was empty. It had not been slept in. It took a moment for this to penetrate his mind. He had heard the others come in during the night and had assumed Juan had returned with them. Perhaps Clint had slept more than he realized. As he lay puzzling this, he heard Monte roll over and come awake. Clint made no move as he watched the old man look over the room from long habit. He, too, stopped at the sight of Juan's empty bed. Monte sat upright, swung his thin legs over the edge of the bed, and dressed quickly to hurry outside to the barn to see if the Mexican's saddle and equipment were there. When he returned in a few moments, he found Clint up and dressed but Bud was still asleep.

"He must not have come home with Bud after all," Monte said. "I heard Bud come in shortly after I did and I was so danged sleepy I just figured Juan was with him."

"Maybe he just quit."

"Never!" exclaimed Monte. "Juan would never run out on the Majors. He must have decided to stay in town with some of his *primos*. He'll be showing up pretty soon."

"It seems funny," Clint persisted evenly.

"I agree. Well, I'll go on up to the house and start us some breakfast since the womenfolk won't be back out here for a few hours yet."

"I'll jingle horses." Clint put on his hat and headed for the corrals.

Monte shook Bud awake and then went to the house. He built a fire in the big range, made the sourdough biscuits, cooked oatmeal, and fried bacon—all was ready when Bud came sleepily into the kitchen. Clint was not back with the horses so the two men ate their meal and sat for some time drinking coffee while waiting for him to come in. Finally, Monte could stand it no longer. He put on his hat and walked slowly to the corrals. There was still no sign of Clint. Monte could not understand what could be holding up the wrangler. As a rule, it was only a matter of minutes for a good cowboy like Clint to bring the horse herd in. There was no place in their horse pasture where the horses could hide for long and it was quite unlikely they had gotten out. The old cowboy climbed the highest corral fence to have a better look, but he could see no sign of a dust cloud that would indicate moving horses.

Monte walked slowly back to the house where he made another pot of coffee to go with the numerous brown-paper cigarettes he smoked. The old man paced the floor constantly as they waited. They were drinking their third cup of strong black coffee when Monte went to the window and saw the wagon coming over the rim of the basin. It must be Becky and her party coming from town. There did not appear to be any riders with the wagon, so Juan must not be returning with them. There was plenty of time for them to finish their coffee before the wagon drew near enough for them to make out the people on the seats.

Monte and Bud walked slowly to the big yard gate and opened it so the team could be driven right up to the kitchen door for unloading the supplies Becky and Helen would be sure to bring. Little Harvey and Susan jumped from the wagon and raced to the house, banging the kitchen door behind them.

"How come you're still around here?" Becky asked, puzzlement in her voice and brown eyes. Normally, the men would have been riding for some hours at this time. "Has something happened?"

"I'm not sure yet, Becky," Monte told her, shrugging his thin shoulders. "Juan didn't come home last night, for one thing. Did you see him in town?"

"No. That is, not after the party. Of course, I thought he came back with you."

"Well, he didn't. Now, Clint must have broken a leg or somethin', for he left to jingle the horses hours ago and hasn't gotten back. Did you see any sign of him as you drove in?"

"No," Frank said from the high seat of the wagon. "I seen the saddle horses way off in the south end of the pasture, but there sure wasn't any rider with them."

"I can't understand that," Monte said. "Bud, unhook the team. You and I'll saddle them and go see what's happened."

"Wait a minute!" exclaimed Frank, who now stood on the front seat of the wagon and was looking back toward the horse pasture. "I think I see something out there. If it's a man, he's leading his horse, not riding it."

Monte quickly scrambled over the wheel and onto the back seat. He shaded his eyes with his hand.

"By God, it does look like Clint, all right, and he's leading his horse. Looks to me like that horse is packing something, though, don't it to you, Frank, more than just a saddle, I mean?"

"You may be right, Monte, but I can't tell from here," Carlson said, smiling. "My eyes aren't as young as yours."

Later, when the man drew closer, making his way through the sagebrush, they could all make out there was indeed something rather large and bulky across his saddle, and the man turned often to see that it was riding all right. As one, they walked toward the big yard gate to meet him. While he was still some ways off, they recognized what was across the saddle—a man's body. Monte let out a grunt and both he and Becky ran forward to help Clint.

It was Juan. Clint led his horse through the gate and to the door of the house without stopping to say a word. He dropped the bridle reins and started to take the man down.

"Help him, Bud," Becky instructed.

"Bud ain't touching him!" Clint said firmly and turned swiftly toward them. Becky stopped in shock.

"What do you mean I'm not going to touch him?" Bud demanded.

Clint stood easily, crouched ever so slightly, as the big man stepped toward him. It was plain to them all Clint was going to fight Bud if he tried to step past him to get to Juan. Bud stopped a few feet from the cowboy, not sure just what he should do next.

"You did this to Juan," Clint spat out, cold hate plain in his voice. "You get your gear and get off this ranch. If I ever find you near the Major outfit again, I'll kill you!"

"I wish you had a gun on right now," Bud challenged. "If you would put one on, we'd see who would do what. You can't prove I done that to Juan."

"I'll take Clint's word for it!" Monte snapped and the sound of his pistol being cocked came from close behind Bud. "Clint wouldn't say that, if he didn't know it. You just keep your hand away from your gun, Bud. Frank, take his pistol and go with him to get his stuff from the bunkhouse. As soon as we can get the horses in, we'll see he leaves with no more trouble."

"You ain't the boss here," Bud stammered, but kept his hands high as Frank took the pistol from his holster.

"With this .45 in my hand, I am," Monte growled.

"I'll get your pay, Bud. You are fired," Becky stated firmly.

As soon as Frank left with the big rider, Monte and Clint carried Juan into the house. He was alive, but not by much. He had been beaten terribly. They did what they could for him, then made ready to send him back to town with Frank in the wagon.

"How did you know Bud did this, Clint?" Becky asked as they were making Juan as comfortable as they could on a mattress in the back of the wagon. "He never came to enough to tell you."

"Bud's ring," Clint answered, "makes kind of an X mark where it hits. It's lucky I found him. I guess his horse must have tried to bring him home and he fell off in the horse pasture."

As he spoke, the cowboy fingered his lip where that same mark had been not too long ago. He would not forget that mark.

A few minutes later the wagon drove off and Frank turned back one more time to wave. It was all Becky could do to force her hand up in return. His wife waved her handkerchief and turned toward the house, her mind already on the things she had to do that day.

"As if we didn't have enough trouble," she said over her shoulder to no one in particular. "Lucky we got Vance off to Ojo this morning before he heard about this. He would never have gone had he known about Juan. It was all we could do to get him to go as it was," Helen lamented. "He is so depressed thinking he's let us all down but we just couldn't let him stay. The doctor is so sure another month in that pool will save his foot."

"And now there are three," Becky said dejectedly. "From five to three in one day."

Clint looked down at her golden hair and the sun-browned skin of her face and neck. Damn it, he thought, he just couldn't ride off and leave her after this, no matter what she thought of him or how she treated him. He knew he would still have to look himself in the face. Slowly, he walked to the night horse and returned to the pasture for the saddle horses.

CHAPTER 10

BECKY changed into her usual riding clothes, while Monte kept an eye on Bud Jarvis at the corrals and waited for Clint to return with the saddle horses. Not wanting to join the two men at the corrals because she did not wish to speak to Bud again, Becky walked slowly along the path to the bunkhouse. She did not usually go there for it was off-limits, so to speak, for females. In fact, she could not remember when she had last seen the inside of that house. The thought came to her that perhaps she should check to make sure Bud had gotten all his things, for she did not want him returning later on an excuse of having left something.

As a precaution, she knocked on the door before entering, even though she knew there could be no one inside. Cowboys were not always a clean group of men; however, the ones who rode on the Major outfit kept the bunkhouse clean and in some order or Monte would soon send them packing. Her brothers had always said Monte was as bad as an old woman about keeping the place neat and clean. She marveled, as she always did, to find the beds neatly made and the men's belongings hung on the walls or in their war sacks under their beds. It took a moment for her to realize only two of the beds had belongings hanging above them. Monte's, of course, and Juan's. She did not know which bed Clint used, but she could see no sign of the sandy-haired cowboy's articles around any of the empty beds. It was then as she turned to leave, still pondering this, she saw the war sack standing near the door, packed and ready for its owner.

She knew immediately it was Clint's. This Clint was an unusual man, proud perhaps beyond measure. She wondered again where he had come from and why he was drifting around the country—he did not act at all like the homeless cowboys who followed the cattle seasons over the western United States. She had seen many of that kind come and go on the ranch. Clint Austin did not fit that pattern, and she knew he had intended to leave this morning.

She was sorry she had offended him after all he had done to help them. Still, she had her pride, too. If they had not been so short-handed, she would let him ride on without any attempt to stop him. Of course, she would have to tell him she had not meant the insult of last night—she had really intended to dance with him. She would tell him all this—no matter what—for that would be the only way she could satisfy her own conscience.

She heard the horses coming and left the bunkhouse before Clint drove the ramuda around the corrals to where he could see her. As she walked toward the corrals, she recalled the day Clint had shot Flack's hat from his head after the Farr foreman had insulted her. Remembering this, she realized she had not been fair to think of letting Clint just ride off. He had gone out of his way for her, even put himself in danger. The very least she could do was make sure he understood what she intended last night. She would not insist he stay, but she knew she owed him an explanation.

Not much was said at the corrals that morning. Bud caught his personal horse, threw his saddle and belongings on it and rode from the ranch under the watchful eye of both Clint and Monte. As soon as the man was well out of sight, she had them catch and saddle the two old cow ponies Vance's children rode when at the ranch. Becky knew they would want to go riding later in the day. Then Becky sent Monte to check one part of their range while she and Clint rode together toward another. They rode in silence for several miles, Clint keeping his horse a half length behind hers. Suddenly, the woman swung her horse and stopped where she could face the man.

"Clint, you misunderstood my intentions last night," she began, hating the quiver that came to her voice. As usual, he said nothing. "I meant only to tell you my father always had that rule but that I certainly did not agree with it or intend to abide by it in your case. You have been different from the kind of puncher the rule was intended for, and I would have been very glad to have danced with you . . . had you not left without letting me finish."

Tears were in her brown eyes as she turned her horse away from him. She was glad she had said it, and she was glad it was over. For a moment they sat there, each holding his horse to a stand. Then the man's drawl came in that quiet way he had.

"I guess I should have known you didn't really feel that way. After all, you work on this ranch the way no other woman I know would do. I'm sorry, Becky. I made a big mistake to judge you so.

"Let's forget it," she said, turning to look at him through tears still in her eyes. "I'm sorry, too, Clint, because I'd not hurt your feelings for anything. It was my fault—for some reason I wanted to tease you and it just didn't come out right."

He smiled at her and slowly shook his head.

"I know you planned to leave today, too," she added.

"I kind of changed my mind again after I found Juan," the man drawled and shifted his weight to rest on one straight leg. "It didn't seem quite right to ride off and leave you and Monte here all alone . . . and I made up my mind Bud was leaving. I must be getting weak-willed in my old age; I've changed my mind a dozen times about leaving . . . and that ain't like me at all."

She returned his smile and they rode on across the prairie, the cowboy now riding beside her. They rode hard that day and covered much of their western range. The Major cattle seemed peaceful and they found but a few strays, not enough to bother to try to gather and push out. Perhaps their luck had turned for the better, the woman thought as they were returning to the ranch late in the afternoon. Dusk was only a short time away when they rode over the crest of the big basin and could see the ranch buildings in the distance. As they neared the house, they made out the figure of someone waving frantically at them from the ranch yard and horses were milling around the corrals. Instantly, they urged their horses to a lope. As they drew closer, they made out the figure to be Helen, her frantic waving making them spur their mounts to a run.

"What in the world has happened now, Helen?" Becky called as they slid their horses to a stop at the wire fence, across from the excited woman.

"It's Susan!" exclaimed the all but hysterical Helen. "She and Little Harvey went riding this afternoon and she hasn't come back!"

"Didn't they ride together?"

"They started out together, as always, but I guess they quarreled about where to go. Little Harvey thinks she may have gone up along the creek toward the Old Ranch to look for arrowheads, or maybe over toward the Big Spring. Little Harvey and I went up the creek quite a ways looking for her, but we didn't see a sign of her and I'm worried. She should have been home hours ago as it's getting dark. The children have never done anything like this before."

"Oh, Lord!" exclaimed Becky. "Vance will never forgive me if I let anything happen to her. Where's Monte?"

"He's at the corral saddling a fresh horse."

"We'll find her," Becky said, trying to calm her sister. "Clint, please take my horse and saddle a fresh one for me, as well as one for yourself. I'll get some lanterns from the house."

"Bud Jarvis may have come back and snatched her just to get even with you," Helen cried, turning to follow Becky inside.

This startling possibility had not occurred to Becky. Bud

might just do such a thing. Now that the idea was in her mind, she found it hard to push aside.

A few minutes later the three riders left the corrals, Monte to go toward the Big Spring, the other two to ride the creek toward the Old Ranch. They only had two lanterns—Becky took one and Monte the other.

At the creek, Becky took the near bank while Clint crossed the almost dry stream to follow the opposite bank. Over the years the floods and winds had cut the sides of this stream into an arroyo with high, steep banks. In some places, this arroyo was over one hundred yards across or as much as twenty-five feet deep. At other spots, the banks would not be over thirty feet apart or over five feet high. In addition to the main arroyo, many smaller washes branched from each side and the riders had to continually circle away from the stream to find a way across them. They had to watch the tricky banks for many of them were unsafe to ride near their edge. At places, the wind and water had eroded big holes under the edge of the banks, some undermined so much they formed natural dirt bridges across the branch arroyos. While some of these bridges were strong enough to hold a man on a horse, most cowboys seldom trusted them, preferring to go the long way around. Becky and Clint were often more than a quarter mile apart as they worked their way up the creek.

Clint forced the young cow pony he rode to hold a steady lope most of the way to the Old Ranch, which was several miles up the creek from the house. There was nothing left of the buildings, merely a pile of dirt and rotting timber. The rider waited there a few minutes, thinking Becky would soon show up. His eyes searched the country on the far side of the arroyo for sight of Becky's lantern, but he could see nothing moving in that direction. He was about to reach the conclusion she had gotten to this spot ahead of him and had gone on to cut across country toward the Big Spring, when his horse suddenly threw up its head and whinnied. The animal must have caught scent or sound of Becky's horse, Clint thought. Again, he turned to look through the rapidly falling darkness in the direction she should be coming from. As he sat there looking across the arroyo, an answer to his horse's whinny came to his ears but it seemed very faint and queer. The sound seemed to come from down the creek in the direction he had just come, and he didn't think it could have been made by Becky's horse.

"Susan! Susan!" He cupped his hands and called the girl's name again and again.

No answer. He turned his horse toward the arroyo bank and started following it back downstream. After he had gone perhaps a hundred yards, his horse whinnied again, and the answer came from the shadows ahead of him. It was a funny, pitiful nicker, and the man's nerves grew taut at the sound.

Although the sun was now completely down, it was still light enough for him to make out the rough, uneven banks of the arroyo. He strained his eyes to watch the tricky edges ahead of his horse. The man stood in his stirrups and cupped his hands to his mouth to call the girl's name as loudly as he could. This time, he heard her answer, a frightened call coming faintly from the stillness ahead of him. It was more a scream than a call and he spurred his horse forward.

A long, deep wash appeared directly ahead of him where a branch joined the main arroyo. As he drew up to the edge the nicker of a horse came from below. The rider leaped to the ground and peered over the edge. Some ten or twelve feet below him was the girl and her horse. The animal was a crumpled heap wedged tightly between the narrow banks where it emptied into the main arroyo, completely filling the hole under the adobe arch bridge across the mouth of the wash. The child stood next to the horse and he saw the girl's left foot was trapped between the saddle and the bank. Both of the horse's front legs were broken but it kept struggling with its hind legs, which only wedged it tighter. The girl was half standing against the bank and half standing on the horse, her eyes full of tears.

Then, in the twilight, Clint saw the snake. It was a rattler, stretched out, not coiled, but only a few feet from the terrified girl. The serpent's forked tongue flicked out incessantly. There were no rocks or sticks handy on the top of the bank. He thought of his rifle but instantly decided he could not risk shooting that near the girl. A glancing bullet might strike her.

Without thinking, he jumped. Luckily, the reptile must not have heard him, for it made no attempt to coil itself until he landed a half step behind it. Clint's hand shot down, grasped the rattled tail and swung the serpent high above his head and over the bank. Luckily, the momentum was such that the snake's head missed his hand. Clint's horse was unused to flying snakes and it bolted as the angry rattler sailed over its head. Clint could hear the horse pounding away into the night. The rattler landed in a small sage bush and its angry buzzing came loudly in the still air. From deep in the bank behind them came the faint sound of its mate.

"Did it bite you?" Clint asked harshly, putting his arm around the little girl.

She could not answer but cried hysterically on his chest. Finally, she shook her head.

"Thank God!" he sighed and felt his legs go weak.

Sweat was running down his face from under his hat brim as he knelt down to examine her foot. Her left ankle was pinned tightly between the hard adobe wall of the wash and the saddle. He tore at the bank with his hands but the ground was too hard. From his pocket he drew his stockman's knife and began carefully picking at the dirt. It was rapidly getting too dark to see, and all the while from above them came the angry buzzing of the snake.

"Will he . . . come back?"

Susan's sobs were shorter and further apart now.

"I don't think so," he said soothingly. "Not if he knows

what's good for him. Hold real still, now, I've almost got you out."

By this time he had managed to scrape out a hole large enough for her to remove her foot from behind the saddle. In the gathering darkness, he could not tell how badly it was hurt, but she could not stand to put any weight on it. The old horse lay in the opening into the main arroyo—that way was completely blocked.

"You stand on my hands with your good foot," he instructed. "Balance yourself against the bank and I'll lift you up so you can pull yourself over the top."

"I'm afraid of that snake!" wailed the girl.

"He's on the other side of the wash. You just do as I say and don't worry about him."

Slowly, he lifted her waist high, then to his shoulders, and finally above his head. She steadied herself against the bank until her head and shoulders were above the side. With the aid of a small bush she dragged herself over the top to lie, breathing hard, on the soft, warm prairie earth.

"How will you get up, Clint?" Susan called down to the man.

"I guess I'll just have to play like I'm a cliff dwelling Indian and cut some hand and toe holds. It won't take long."

But Clint was wrong—it took some time for him to hack out enough hand and toe holds so he could mount the vertical bank. Once out, he found the girl shivering on the ground. Again, he tried to examine her foot with his fingers in the darkness. All he could be sure of was the ankle was badly swollen, and she cried out in pain if he pressed it even slightly.

"Well, the worst is over now," he said and helped her stand on her good foot. "We can make it home just fine from here. I'll kneel down and you climb up on my shoulders. That way, I can carry you all the way home. That dang horse of mine would run off."

"I'm so glad you found me, Clint," she sobbed, as he knelt

down in front of her. "I thought no one would find me in time."

The child's words touched him deeply. He helped her get settled on his shoulders then slowly stood up.

"You just try to forget what happened," he advised, as he started the long walk back to the ranch. "Your aunts will be worried to death about you before I can get you home." A moment later he could not help but add, "I'm sure glad I found you, too, Susan."

Becky crossed the arroyo a short distance above the Old Ranch. It was dark now and there was still no sign of Susan. Fear made her urge her horse to a faster pace as she left the creek and headed across country toward the Big Spring. She saw no sign of Clint and assumed he had already started toward the spring since he had had the shorter side of the creek to ride. All the worry and tension of the past months seemed to heap upon her as she rode. The only real love and devotion Vance allowed in his life centered on his two children. If anything serious had happened to Susan, it would be more than Vance could bear and Becky knew she would always feel responsible. She could not hold back the thought that perhaps Bud had come back and taken the little girl. There would be nothing he could do worse than that to get even with her for firing him.

In the eastern sky, the moon was peeking over the horizon, and before long it would shed a little light over the country-side. The night breeze was also coming up and it chilled her through her light shirt. She shivered and mentally pictured the little girl lying on the prairie with the cold breeze blowing over her. It was not a pleasant thought and she tried to drive it from her mind. With pressing spurs, she forced her horse to hold its swift pace. She held the lantern as high as she could and tried to keep her eyes moving all the time to see as much ground as possible. Clint must be ahead of her somewhere and she wanted to catch up with him if she could.

However, before she had gone halfway from the creek to the Big Spring, which was a good seven or eight miles, she met Monte. The old cowboy had seen nothing of either the girl or Clint.

"Maybe he found her," Monte suggested.

"He had his rifle and I told him to fire a shot to let us know. I didn't hear any shot," Becky said, her feelings showing in her tight voice.

"Well, maybe he found her and decided to go back to the ranch and not wait for us. He could even have fired a shot or two and the way you were riding, you'd not have heard it. Hell, she may even have gotten home under her own power by this time."

Monte didn't really believe this, she knew, but he was trying to help her keep up her hopes.

"I only hope she's all right."

"Why don't you head out for the house and I'll go back around the long way just in case Clint was behind you," Monte suggested.

They split up there and forced their mounts to a slow lope. At the ranch, Becky found the lights blazing and her sister almost out of her mind with worry. Neither Susan nor Clint had been there. Becky was frantic. She took but enough time to refill the lantern before swinging back into the saddle.

This time she went up the side of the arroyo that Clint had gone before. With each movement of the trotting horse, her mind was praying, let us find her. She swung the lantern to inspect each draw and cut. Please let us find her all right. Clouds were now drifting across the moon's path and much of its light was blotted out. She covered half the distance to the Old Ranch without any sign of either the girl or the cowboy.

Then, a shout came floating from the darkness ahead of her and her heart leaped within her breast. She spurred her horse ahead, answering the call. At length, she saw the ghostly figure of the girl riding high on the shoulders of the slender cowboy as they came into the circle of yellow light from her lantern. At the sight, her horse shied and almost jumped from under her. The only thing Becky could think of was Susan must be all right, for she was smiling and waving to her. The child's smile went right to her aunt's heart and gave it a tug she would never forget.

Swiftly, Becky was off her horse and at Clint's side as he knelt down to lift the girl gently from his shoulders. Becky gathered the child into her arms and cuddled her tightly to her breast to cover her own shaking nerves.

"Oh, Susan, are you all right?"

"Only my foot's hurt a little," the girl said.

"Thank God! Thank God!"

A minute later, Becky drew her pistol and fired a shot into the air to signal Monte and Helen that the girl had been found. Moments later, an answering shot drifted back through the still night air from far up the creek where Monte had been searching.

"Will your horse ride double?" Clint asked Becky.

"I think he will."

He lifted the girl to the saddle and held the animal while Becky swung up behind her.

"Do you want to try to ride, too?" Becky asked. "I don't think he'd object."

"No thanks. I'll just walk on in."

Becky left him the lantern and turned the horse toward home. They soon melted into the darkness ahead of the man. Susan felt she could stand the bouncing of a gallop, so they rode swiftly toward the blazing lights of the ranch house.

"Clint's the bravest man I ever saw," the girl said over her shoulder as Becky finally drew the horse to a walk.

"As brave as your daddy or Uncle Harvey?"

"Yes, sir, just as brave!" Susan said positively. "You should have seen him jump down and grab that old rattlesnake by the tail with his bare hands!"

"Snake?"

Susan then told her aunt the whole story. As the girl talked, Becky's mind went back to Clint somewhere behind them in the darkness of the prairie night. It seemed this man constantly became more important to her. As long as she lived, she would never forget him coming into that circle of light from her lantern with the little girl riding high on his shoulders. Suddenly, she realized she had never felt about any man the way she was now feeling toward this one.

Happiness reigned supreme at the ranch house now that the girl was safely home. Her foot was not seriously hurt. As she ate the meal Aunt Helen had saved for her, she told them the story of what had happened. She had not been paying proper attention to where she was riding, looking down at the ground for arrowheads, and the old horse had gotten too close to a bank. It caved off with them before she even realized what had happened.

Clint's horse had returned to the corrals and Monte was about to take him back to the cowboy when Clint walked through the yard gate.

"That's sure not my natural means of locomotion," he drawled ruefully. "Don't remember when I walked that far. Don't turn my horse out, Monte. I'll have to go back up there and put that old horse out of his misery. If I'd had a gun I'd have done it while I was there."

Monte had broken that horse and had ridden him many years before he was more or less retired to be used only by the children.

"It wouldn't be right to let him suffer," Monte said softly. "However, let me go and take care of that chore."

"Thanks, Monte, but I know right where he is. You might not be able to find him in the dark. I will take a lantern and a gentle horse to bring back the saddle and bridle."

Monte shook his head sadly, knowing Clint was right.

After Clint had ridden into the night on his errand of mercy, Monte slowly unsaddled his and Becky's horses and turned them out for the night. He wasn't sure his old legs were going to carry him all the way to the house, but they did, protesting at each step. He didn't think he was interested in any supper but he sure needed some of Helen's coffee. However, after a bite or two of the food, it seemed to taste pretty good after all.

Over an hour later a very tired and weary Clint Austin dismounted stiffly at the corrals, his mission of mercy accomplished. He unsaddled the horses and led them to the pasture gate.

"You son of a gun," he chided his horse mildly as he slipped the bridle. "If you ever leave me afoot that way again, I'm gonna get something and pound some sense into your head."

A sound came from behind him and he was startled, spinning around. He knew he had been tired but he wasn't aware he was so tired anyone could get that close to him without his hearing them. The thought provoked him.

"You still up, Miss Major?"

"I wanted you to know how much we appreciate what you did, Clint," the woman said and stepped up beside him.

"Oh, well, that ain't at all necessary," he replied rather shortly. "I'm just thankful I found her."

"You're a very brave man, Clint. Not many would have jumped down on that snake, as Susan said you did. How in the world did you manage to keep from being bitten?"

"Well, I was moving just as fast as I could," the man drawled, stepping back from her a little to see her face better in the moonlight. "I reckon that snake was looking so hard at Susan he just plum forgot to protect his rattles."

"I just kept praying Susan would be safe," Becky said then, and was immediately surprised at his response.

"I've been told that prayer solves a lot of problems."

"Why, I didn't realize you were a church man, Clint." Her surprise was in her voice.

"I'm just a cowboy, Becky. No self-respecting church would

have anything to do with me. I don't know much about God—I had no one to teach me since I left home in Texas as a boy. However, I don't see how anyone can deny there is a God. After looking up at the stars and thinking of all the wonders of this world, you some way know there has to be someone up there running things," the man said softly.

She had never heard him speak this way, and suddenly she realized this man, usually so reserved when around her, was laying before her some of his innermost feelings.

"I once had a friend," he continued, "a man I rode for and think the world of, and he had a great faith in God. He didn't go around praying or bragging but he tried to live his faith. That's the kind of man I want to be. I know one more thing, too. If I ever should be lucky enough to find a woman who would have me, I want her to be a Christian. I don't want my children growing up to know nothing of God, the way I did."

As he spoke, Clint looked down at her in the moonlight. Here was the woman he had dreamed of. In his heart, he knew he loved her, that he had for some time. However, his convictions were strong; no drifting cowboy would ever win her heart and he had nothing to offer. Gallantly, he held out his arm, which she took gently, and he walked her back to the house. There was no more thought of leaving. He knew he would never leave her until all the things at the ranch were back to normal, no matter what happened.

CHAPTER 11

THE next day brought a serious discovery. Not only had a large number of Cameron and Payne cattle been pushed onto their range during the night, but also Monte suspected fifty head or more of their steers were missing. They spent the rest of the day trying to prove it but by evening they still were not sure. The days dragged into weeks and each day became a nightmare of hard riding. The fact they were losing ground every day just made them work harder, always pressing to catch up with what now seemed impossible. They could not keep up this pace forever. As Monte said, "It's like trying to throw your saddle on a whirlwind."

They got a letter from Vance saying his foot was beginning to mend. However, the doctors would not allow him to return home, as they still feared his foot would get worse again if he stopped the treatments too quickly.

One morning they awoke to find the weather had changed. There were low clouds overhead, and a steady drizzle of rain was falling as they rode, hunched in their slickers. They checked the cattle in the Big Spring pasture and found comparatively few strays. This was the first time in weeks a fresh group of outside cattle had not been pushed in on them. From the Big Spring, they rode the drift fence, which ran several miles along the northwest end of the range they considered theirs. At a fence gate, Monte discovered tracks of about fifty head of cattle having been pushed out of their pasture. For a few moments, the three sat quietly on their horses and looked off across the fence. Someone had definitely taken cattle out of their pasture through that gate.

"Who owns that land?" Clint asked.

"Farr owns about two sections lying along the big draw there," Becky answered. "It don't connect with any of his other holdings and he has let Russ Payne lease it from him for several years. Russ has a place that joins it on the left. It don't amount to much as it's pretty rough."

"The country gets a darn sight rougher on to the north," Clint concluded, looking off into the distance. He had crossed some of that country just a few months ago.

"I'll say it does," Monte assured him. "There is some of the worst badlands in New Mexico up there. It's really fit for nothing. However, the Bennetts and a few other fast-rope artists have located in a few canyons with some feed and water. There ain't many."

It had now stopped raining, and Clint stepped from his horse to pull off his slicker before opening the gate. The others also pulled their slickers and tied them behind their saddles. Clint had a little trouble making the buckskin he rode stand while he tied the slicker. He had taken over some of the horses Juan had ridden—the best mounts on the ranch. This big, strong buckskin was a fine horse but still young and inexperienced. Today had been the first time anyone had ridden him with a slicker.

"Is there another fence before the badlands?" Clint asked as he walked to the gate.

"Yes. There's a gate right up this draw," Monte told him and lifted his arm to point toward the higher ground. "You can see the fence coming off the high point on the right."

"Well, what do you think we should do?" Becky asked.

"I'll bet those were our cattle that went through this gate," Monte stated flatly. "Let's take a look."

"Bunch of riders coming toward us from the left," Clint said a moment later, as his roving eyes missed little, especially when it moved.

"They look like they're coming from Russ Payne's," Monte said. "Let's just sit tight and see what they have to say."

They had to wait some time for the five riders as they slow-walked their horses toward them. When the men drew close enough, they recognized Bud Jarvis and Emil Watson riding in the lead. Russ Payne and Sid Cameron trailed behind them with another cowboy. Watson's long face was plainly marked forever by Clint's rope. The man never let his eyes waver from Clint Austin but he said nothing.

"What do you think you're going to do, Monte?" Bud Jarvis asked belligerently as they drew rein in front of the Major riders. "In case you was thinkin' of coming through that gate, I'd take another think. This is Farr land and no Major is going to set foot on it while I work for Mr. Farr."

"So you're riding for Farr now," Monte said and added, "Didn't know Farr was that hard up for help."

"Watch your tongue, old man!" Bud snapped. "I ain't only riding for him, I'm assistant foreman. I'm running this part of the operation."

"I think it has always been customary for any neighbor to be allowed on your place to look for strays," Becky said evenly. "You can see cattle have been driven through this gate during the rain last night or early this morning. We'd like to see where they went and whose they were."

"Why, we gathered some of Russ and Sid's stuff out of your place yesterday, just like you asked us to," Bud said, hastily looking at the tracks. "Ain't that right, Russ?"

"Why . . . sure. Must have been forty, fifty head we brought back in here."

"Where did you take them?" Monte asked sarcastically. "Besides, those tracks weren't made yesterday. They was made early this morning."

"Well, it really ain't any of your business what we did with the cattle. We drove them all the way back to Russ's pasture," Bud said, eyeing Monte closely.

The white-haired old cowboy rubbed his chin thoughtfully. "Sure strange," he muttered.

"What's strange?"

"Most people getting those cows through that gate in the

rain would have just dropped them on that grass," Monte mused. "Ain't it kind of strange you took them all the way home to Russ's beat-out old pasture through the rain when, last we heard, Russ was leasing this grass from Farr anyway. You fellows sure must like to punch cows in the rain."

"Well, we did just that," Bud growled.

"Sure strange, too, you took them the long way around in that rain," the old man continued. "Them tracks lead right straight up the draw in place of turning south towards Russ's pasture. Sure is a strange way to take them . . . but then you was probably fightin' rain so hard you couldn't see where they was goin' . . . especially since you must have done it in the dark."

"Well, by God, we got them there anyway!" Bud shouted in anger.

" 'Course you did, Bud. Why, even with old Russ there riding point and knowing where home was, you took them miles out of your way just to have a nice ride in the rain and the dark. Does seem kinda strange to me."

"You think what you want, Monte." Bud knew his lies had not fooled the old man for an instant. "But you ain't been friendly about our cows on your land and we ain't gonna let you come on ours."

"Let's go, Monte," Clint drawled.

The slender cowboy turned the buckskin away from the fence and the other riders slowly followed.

"Don't try coming back this way!" Bud called. "We're gonna stick around to see you don't."

The cowboy with Payne dismounted and closed the gate.

Clint put the buckskin into a long trot and led the others swiftly away from the fence. After he had gone some way, he slowed the horse until the others caught up with him.

"Got an idea?" Monte asked, sensing something about Clint's attitude.

"Do you really think those were our cows that went through that gate?" Clint asked.

"I'll bet my life on it," Monte said with a snort. "Bud was lying in his teeth trying to cover up for somebody. If they didn't push those cows through there, he knows who did."

"I can't see Farr taking such a chance as stealing someone's cows," Clint said.

"I doubt he did, or knew it if his men did," Monte said slyly. "However, Smokey Bennett used to run cows off into those badlands where he could change a brand on them. That's how Harvey caught him and sent him to the pen. I've wondered ever since we first thought someone was running off some of our stock if Smokey had started up operations again. Farr probably wouldn't steal a cow but he could sure cover Smokey's back trail. With Russ and Sid pushing their stuff on us and Smokey stealing ours, everything would work out in Farr's favor without him actually doing anything himself."

"You're probably right, Monte. Those tracks sure weren't headed for Payne's." Clint drew his horse to a halt as they were now out of earshot of the Farr riders. "Do you think you might catch up with the cows if I drew those riders off?"

"How would you do that?"

"I'll ride up the fence beyond that ridge a ways, then cut the fence. I'll stay behind the ridge until I get up to about where those cedars are on the skyline. Then I'll show myself as though I'm looking for tracks going toward Payne's. I think if you ride on away from here, that whole bunch will take off after me. When they do, I'll lead them on a merry chase and you can come back and follow those tracks."

"It might work, but it's risky," Monte agreed. "There's another gate in that fence about a mile south of the one we were at. I'd go to it and not cut the fence."

"They might shoot you," Becky objected.

"I think this buckskin can outrun their horses," Clint stated. "If not, I've got my rifle and they know I'll use it if they push me too hard. You're the ones to take care. If you find the cattle and they're ours, don't take any chances on getting shot trying to get them back. Your brother, Harvey, can do that later. Whoever took them will probably drop them somewhere for a day or two before attempting to work over the brands anyway, so you'll probably find the cattle and no riders."

"I think you're right. We do need to get those cows if they're ours. We've lost too many already," Monte stated.

"Well, I'll see if I can't lead those boys away so you can see what you'll find. I'll see you back at the ranch some time tonight."

"It might be better if I led them off," Monte said slowly. "I know the country better than you. If they force you into the badlands they could box you in."

"I'll make out. Besides, I've got the rifle and the fastest horse."

Clint left them then and trotted the buckskin on an angle back toward the fence. Becky let her eyes follow the slender shape standing in the stirrups. Monte spurred his horse to a trot directly away from the fence and the Farr riders. These men now all turned to watch the man on the buckskin.

"What do you suppose he's up to?" Russ Payne growled and spat tobacco juice from the side of his large mouth.

"He's probably just going up along the fence," Bud said. "The rest of them are heading home."

"Keep your eyes on Austin," Watson advised. "I'll bet he's up to something."

The men sat on their horses and watched the buckskin as it went away from them at a long swinging trot.

"That dun horse is a darn good animal," Bud said, rubbing his black beard. "Juan always said he was fast and had lots of staying power."

Clint now dropped over the rolling prairie out of sight of the men, yet they continued to watch just in case he showed up again farther down the fence line. He did not. This puzzled them and without comment they let their horses drift along the fence in the direction Clint had taken. Some time later, it was Watson's roving eye that caught the movement of the buckskin against the skyline far to their right. The horse stopped under the cedars for a moment.

"There he is! Look up there on the ridge on your right," the gunman snarled. "Hell, he's trying to circle around us and check on those tracks."

"Let's teach him a lesson!" Bud shouted and spurred his horse into a run. "He's on Farr land now and we've got him where we want him."

The other four men spurred to keep up with the big man. Watson snapped a shot at the rider with his pistol, knowing the distance was so great it would be a miracle if he even came close.

From his chosen spot on the crest of the rolling ridge, Clint watched the men below. Watson's eye had been quick to spot him. He waited until he saw all five riders coming toward him, then reined his horse around and dropped over the crest. Even as he moved, a spent pistol bullet cut through the branches of one of the cedars. He was glad he had his rifle—an advantage if things got tough.

The buckskin was still fresh and he let him out to try to stay out of pistol range. The terrain was rough and cut with rocky ridges and gullies. It took all his skill as a horseman just to stay in the saddle as the horse jumped, dodged, and turned as they headed across country. In spite of the roughness, he managed to keep the animal headed almost directly away from the men behind him. They would have a difficult time circling to get ahead of him. After some distance, he pulled the horse down to a trot, not wanting to waste its strength, for this could be a long chase. The best he could expect, if caught, would be a beating.

A few minutes later, a bullet whistled over his head as he ducked around the point of a small hill. One of the men was trying to flank him. So far, he could not tell if they were trying to scare him with those shots, or were actually trying to hit him. The country was too rough, and his horse was moving too fast for him to even think of attempting to return their fire. If it came to that, he would stop and make his shots count.

A fence suddenly loomed directly ahead and the buckskin slid to a stop before hitting it; in this position, the horse could not jump. Clint leaped from the saddle and kicked savagely at the wires until they were loose from the post and he could hold them down to lead the horse across. He swung back into his saddle and put the horse up the side of a sloping gully at an angle to the way he had been going. Moments later, another shot drew blood across his horse's rump. It did no serious harm, but it told him they meant business. Well, two could play that game, he thought, if he had to, but five to one were pretty long odds.

On and on he fled, pushing deeper into the badlands, always dodging and circling. Each decision he made was a chance. Not knowing the country, he never knew if a turn would lead to country he could get through, or if it would turn out to be a dead end. He tried to keep working toward his right, as he felt there were likely to be less flankers on that side and he would be less apt to run into riders from one of the other ranches. If he could outride the flankers, he could circle the other way and get back to the ranch. He kept trying to remember the country from his ride there several months ago. Funny how little he remembered.

Suddenly, he came out of a draw and into a small group of cattle, which scattered in fright before him. His quick eye caught the brand. They were part of the missing Major cattle, although not the ones that had been moved last night. These had been in the badlands for several weeks.

Noon came and passed and still he rode, never stopping. Now, he rode mostly at a trot ˀnding in the stirrups and trying to watch in all directioı.ɔ. There were no sounds or signs of pursuit anymore. Once, late in the afternoon, he did see two riders a great distance off to his right on top of a high knoll. He did not know if they were some of the men after him, or if they saw him.

He was coming out of the rougher country and back to better grassland. He came to a fence and again kicked the wires loose and led the horse across. Ordinarily, he would have stopped to put the wire back up, but today he remounted and rode on. He knew Sundown must be off somewhere to the south and west of him, and he pushed on toward where he thought it would be. About dusk, he saw the light of a ranch and circled it widely. A little later he came to a well-traveled road and turned on to it.

It was nearly dark when he rode down the main street of the town. The buckskin was near exhaustion and the rider was tired and hungry. A light burned in the window of the sheriff's office and he pulled up in front of it.

Inside the office, he only found a Mexican deputy. Harvey Major was in Santa Fe on business and would not be home for over a week. Clyde Sykes, the only deputy Clint knew personally was also out of town. Clint did not want to discuss the problem with anyone but Harvey, so he asked the deputy to have the sheriff come to the ranch as soon as he returned.

Clint stepped back out to the street in disgust, remembering his friend of long ago saying, "The sheriff is never around when you need him." He led his horse to the livery stable where he finally talked the owner into letting him have a horse to ride back to the ranch. He would leave the buckskin as security until he could get back for him.

After saddling the rental horse, he rode back up the street to where the lights of the cafe were shining brightly. He dismounted and tied the horse at the hitch rail in front of the building.

He had just started up the steps to the sidewalk when the cafe door opened and several men came out. Too late, he recognized Hal Flack and Carl Farr leading them. They all stopped, and for a moment they stood eyeing each other.

"Well, I didn't think you had the guts to come to town

alone," Flack drawled, his cold eyes snapping. "You didn't bring your woman to hide behind."

"I don't remember seeing any sign saying Farr owned this place," Clint replied, his drawl matching the others for coldness.

"Some things are there, even if you can't see them," the Farr foreman told him. Over his shoulder he spoke to his employer. "How about it, Carl?"

"Well, I think now is as good a time as any, Hal," came the reply. "Harvey's out of town. Besides, we've been needing to give this man a lesson. He's messed up our plans about enough."

Clint understood instantly. Without hesitation, Flack moved forward, but Clint moved, too. He sidestepped the foreman as the man lunged off the sidewalk and threw his hip against Flack to send the man off balance. Then, Clint shoved Farr back against the cowboy directly behind the ranch owner. Moving like a flash, Clint caught the fourth man by his throat, forcing him over backward onto the sidewalk. They fell heavily together and Clint brought his knee up to the man's stomach. As the puncher jackknifed, Clint grabbed for the man's pistol, but the cowboy managed to roll over until the gun was beneath his body and Clint could not reach it.

Farr had not gone all the way down, catching himself with the doorjamb. He now drew his pistol from under his coat and lifted it over his shoulder, ready to strike Austin on the head as the cowboy rolled clear of the man beneath him.

Suddenly, the pistol was grabbed from behind Farr and very roughly twisted from his hand, almost taking a finger with it. Flack and the other Farr riders were already moving quickly toward Clint when a man with Farr's Colt at his side stepped from the cafe door and stood between them. It was Tim Harding, the home guard Clint had seen at the Fisher dance. The Farr riders stopped abruptly in stunned surprise.

Carl Farr felt the muzzle of his own pistol pressing against his stomach.

"Seems right unfair," Tim said, his voice very calm. "Four against one. Now, you there on the sidewalk, just keep your hand off that pistol before I blow it off," he admonished the man Clint had knocked down. "There, that's better."

Clint leaned down to remove the man's pistol, which he now also leveled at the Farr riders.

"Now, look here, Harding," Farr blustered. "You're playin' in a game over your head."

He stopped, his eyes wide, as the tall Harding pulled the hammer of the rancher's gun back to full cock.

"Now you just take it easy, Mr. Farr," Tim advised in a pleasant but tight voice. "You're not pushing either of us."

"Look," Flack began, but he, too, stopped short as Clint stepped toward him with pistol at ready.

"All you Farrs drop those pistols and get the hell out of here," Clint instructed.

The men turned slowly and walked down the street. They all looked back to watch the two cowboys shove the guns they had taken away from them into the waistbands of their pants and go into the cafe.

Clint shook his head and stuck his hand out to the tall, young rancher who clasped it in an iron grip. "Thanks, friend. I don't know why you did it, but I'm sure grateful."

"Hell, my dad's been saying for months Farr was probably giving the Majors fits. We heard Becky fired Bud and Juan is in no condition to ride. I just couldn't see letting them lose another hand." Harding turned his head away from Clint and added, "I . . . really think too much of the Majors not to take a hand. I should have gone out long ago."

"I'll tell Becky what you did," Clint said. "Hope you didn't get yourself into a pickle on my account."

"Don't worry about it, Austin. There is nothing in the world Carl Farr wants less than to take on Dad. He knows damn well if that happened, the Majors would be the least of his troubles." Tim moved over to a table and sat down and waved for Clint to join him. "Looks like you had a hard day. I'll wait while you grab a bite and see you safely out of town."

Clint was glad for the company. After he had eaten, Tim got his horse and rode to the edge of town with him. Here he drew rein.

"You should be all right from here," the young man said. "Tell Becky I'll be out sometime tomorrow to lend a hand. We've stayed out of this too long."

"I'll tell her . . . and thanks, again."

Tim lifted his hand and rode off into the night.

Monte had turned back at the sound of Watson's shot and they lifted their horses to a long lope. By the time they got to where they could see the Farr pasture, they caught a glimpse of the riders going over the ridge by the cedars. Monte could see most of the pasture the cattle had gone through and there was no sign of any other riders.

"Let's go," he said curtly and loped his horse to the gate. "Looks like Clint's idea worked. They're all off chasing him."

The old man swung to the ground rather stiffly and opened the gate. Closing it behind them, he swung back into his saddle and they took off again in a lope, following the cattle tracks, which were plainly visible in the soft dirt. About a mile up the wide draw, they came to another fence and gate and went through. Becky breathed a sigh of relief.

"At least we're off Farr's land," she said. "This is open range."

"We're heading right into Bennett country," Monte added. "I ain't too sure which is safer."

The cattle tracks led into the rougher country and they followed them, traveling at a slow trot now that they were safely off Farr's land. The trail led deeper and deeper into the badlands. Little grass grew here in the broken, arroyo-filled country of soft clay hills. It was past noon when they came to a small, well-hidden valley with fair grass and a small spring-fed pond. Here they found their cattle, grazing contentedly, no rider in sight. Monte quickly rode through the herd—they were all Major cattle.

"Shall we just take them home?" Becky asked. "It's a long way back."

"Maybe we ought to go pay Smokey Bennett a visit," Monte suggested. "I think his outfit is just a couple of draws west of here. We should let him know we tracked these cows here and we know what he's up to."

"No," Becky said calmly, but firmly. "Let's get our cows home and I'll have Harvey take care of Smokey Bennett."

"I'm not so sure these cows can travel home. They came a right far piece already," Monte argued.

"They'll go at least part of the way," the woman said and started her horse around the edge of the valley. "Let's get them moving."

Monte could see it was going to be of no use to argue and turned his horse after hers.

A short time after they got back to the ranch in the early hours of the morning, Clint arrived. They were all glad to crawl under their blankets as soon as they could and slept heavily.

Carl Farr and Hal Flack did not sleep so well. After their run-in with Austin, they had ridden to the Farr ranch, only to be met by more disturbing news. Bud Jarvis and his men had chased Austin all across the north end of Payne's spread and lost him in the badlands. Hal Flack's brows narrowed over his eyes as Bud told them of the day's events.

"I'll bet he decoyed you off on purpose," the foreman guessed instantly. "I'll bet Monte and Becky followed those tracks to where Smokey dropped those cows and probably took them home as soon as you were out of sight."

"Oh, I doubt it," Bud denied quickly. "They had already headed back home before we saw Austin sneaking around us."

"Hell, you would never have seen him if he hadn't wanted

you to," Hal insisted. "He suckered you, Bud. I'll bet Monte has those cows home by now and they know just what happened to them."

"This is bad news," Farr snapped. "That damned Harding kid sure spoiled a good thing for us tonight."

"We should have let Waston handle Austin when he first wanted to," Hal said. "Then, we could have gotten away with most anything. Now, if young Harding squeals to his dad, it could be harder to get rid of Austin."

"And, that damn cow market goes up every week," Farr muttered. "Ordinarily I'd be delighted but each time it goes up now, they need to sell fewer cows to meet their payment to me."

"Well, what's the next move?" Flack asked. "If they found their cows and guess Bennett drove them off, they'll be down on him in force."

"Don't you think they'll wait for Harvey?"

"I doubt it. Monte is an old fire eater and this Austin is no fool. They'll move now that they have something to go on— they know they can probably scare Bennett, as he has no crew, only relatives." Farr paced the long living room as he spoke. "They still don't know Smokey is working with us and probably think he was merely taking advantage of the situation. They'll talk big to him, not realizing they are really bucking us."

"Think they can make Smokey talk?" the foreman asked. "I know he don't like the Majors at all, but I'm not too sure how much he likes us."

"I don't doubt Austin and Monte can make him spill all he knows. If they can't, Harvey will when he gets back. Smokey's scared stiff of our sheriff. Hell, Smokey's our one weak link."

"Maybe Watson and I should go have a talk with Smokey," Flack suggested.

"First thing in the morning," the rancher agreed. "It's imperative Smokey doesn't give away our plans. You see to it that he understands."

CHAPTER 12

THE Farr foreman and Emil Watson left the Farr ranch before daybreak. They kept their horses at a steady trot because they wanted to be sure to reach Smokey Bennett's place before anyone from the Major ranch did. Hal Flack had never been to Smokey's ranch, although he knew where it was. Flack also knew how important Bennett's part in his boss's plan had been. He cussed the rustler for being so careless as to move cattle in the rain.

They crossed a corner of Russ Payne's spread and entered the badlands. About midmorning they came to a deep canyon, which ran through most of the badlands. After a moment's consultation, they turned right along the rim of the canyon. They had not gone quite a mile when they found a rough trail winding steeply to the canyon floor; they let their horses pick their way carefully down the trail.

Once in the canyon, they turned up the dry bottom and again lifted their horses to a trot. There was little grass here, but there were occasional pockets of water in the otherwise dry stream bed.

At a spot where the canyon widened they found a small fenced-in meadow where several saddle horses were grazing contentedly next to a creek. A two-track wagon road joined their trail and they followed it around the edge of the little grass meadow. Just above the meadow, hidden in the cedar and piñon trees, was Smokey's cabin, corrals, and sheds. No smoke came from the chimney and there were no horses in the corrals.

A hitching post with a steel ring stood a short distance from the front door of the house. The adobe cabin was not much—run-down and poorly kept. Never had any of the boards seen paint. Hal Flack thought to himself, this is a hell of a place for a woman. He wondered why any woman would stay there with Smokey Bennett. But, you could never tell— Sarah Bennett might actually love the little rustler.

There seemed to be no sign of life. Flack dismounted and handed the reins of his horse to Watson and walked slowly toward the rickety steps that led up to the door. As he moved, his eyes constantly searched the country within his view. Twice he stopped when he thought he caught a movement in the piñon trees that grew against the canyon walls. Each time, however, he decided it must be the breeze that stirred them.

The steps creaked under his weight. He was at the door now and he lifted his left hand and knocked loudly. There was no answer. He knocked again. This time, he thought he heard something move inside the house but he could not be sure.

"Smokey!" he called loudly.

Again, he thought he heard something move slightly in the house but no answer came to his call. Perhaps Mrs. Bennett was alone and afraid to answer the door.

"It's Hal Flack!" he called again. "Are you there, Smokey?"

This time the sound was louder but he could not make out what was causing it. He drew his pistol and rapped on the door with the barrel. The door felt unlocked—it shook when he struck it. Leveling his gun in his right hand, he turned the knob with his left and suddenly swung the door in and open.

What a sight met his eyes! Furniture was strewn all over the room. Clothing and bedding were tossed over everything. Broken dishes were scattered about and the whole room was in shambles. It seemed impossible the Majors could have been here ahead of them but what else could have caused this! Damn it, if Smokey had betrayed them there would be hell to pay.

Then he saw the man. His eyes widened and he stepped inside. Smokey Bennett lay by the overturned sofa, tied tightly with a lariat rope until he could hardly move. A piece of cloth was tied in his mouth as a gag, and he had been beaten with a quirt, which now lay on the floor beside him. He was a mass of welts and blood, his shirt cut to ribbons.

Flack knelt beside the man to untie the ropes and remove the gag. He called Watson and it took both of them several minutes to get the sofa righted and the man stretched out on it. In what had been the kitchen, Flack found the remains of several bottles of whiskey, but he could find none with anything left in it. Even the water bucket had been emptied on the floor.

He picked up the bucket and walked out the back door to the well. A few moments later, when he forced a little of the cool water down Smokey's throat, the man was able to speak.

"Austin really worked you over, didn't he?" Flack asked. "He sure got here fast. Did you tell him anything?"

"Austin, hell!" muttered the little rustler, not much life showing behind his smoke-colored eyes today. "That damn woman done this to me."

"Your wife?"

"That's right. I guess I beat her up once too often." The man's eyes went slowly over the room. "She sure tore things up, didn't she?"

"Well, how in the world did she ever manage to tie you in the first place?" Flack asked, giving the man a little more water.

"After we got in from moving some of Majors' cows in the rain night before last, I'd taken a drink or two. Sometimes, when I had a little too much, I kinda slapped her around a little bit," the rustler told him. "Hell, a man's got the right to make his woman know he's the boss in his own home, don't he?" He was beginning to speak freely now. "I knowed she didn't like it but never figured she had the guts to do anything about it. Anyway, after I'd worked her over a little,

I got so drunk I passed out here on the sofa. She tied me up while I was asleep and I never realized what was happenin' till I came to with her beatin' on me and screaming all kinds of insults and names at me. I think she was right-smart mad."

"Well, I guess so. You look like a wildcat clawed you."

"I couldn't feel any worse if one had," Smokey admitted. "How come you Farrs are out this way?"

"We brought you a little warning," Flack said, a smile on his thin lips. "You got a little careless when you moved those steers in the rain, Smokey. You left tracks a blind man could follow. The Major outfit was on your trail when Bud and a few of our boys wouldn't let them cross the Farr pasture we rent to Payne."

"Mighty neighborly of you."

"This Austin fellow led Bud and his boys on a merry goose chase, and I'll bet old Monte tracked those cows down and took them home."

"What do you figure they'll do? They can't prove I drove them anywhere."

"I kind of doubt this Austin fellow will worry much about proof." Again, Flack smiled thinly. "I'd lay odds he and Monte will be paying you a call before this day is over."

"I'd better go get some of the other Bennett clan rounded up, pronto." Smokey tried to stand but failed.

"Even Becky Major could whip you in your condition," Watson interposed.

"I guess you're right," Smokey said sadly as Flack helped him to his feet. "At least you'll stay here till they come, won't you? I'd be hard put to give much account of myself today."

"I'd like to stay," Watson answered. "I'd like nothing better than to get a chance at Austin."

"Sorry," Flack said, "but we've got to pull out. If we got caught here, they'd know for sure we were working this together. We'll help you on your horse, then you'd better get to some of your relatives and hide out before the Majors find you. Mr. Farr will send you your money in the usual manner as long as you don't tell them anything. If they don't catch up with you, they can't ask embarrassing questions. You understand?"

Everyone at the Major outfit slept a little late that morning. Becky finally forced herself to slide out of bed and into her clothes. She went to the kitchen to start a fire, then returned to her room where she took a few minutes to brush her hair. She had not had time to care for herself as she should lately, and again she could not quiet down the wish that Vance could come home soon.

Helen was up now and Becky heard her sister singing softly as she started the biscuits. Becky went to join her in the chores of getting breakfast ready. A few minutes later they heard the men coming from the bunkhouse.

"I'm sure glad you got back all right," Becky said as Clint entered the kitchen. "How far did they chase you?"

"A right-smart ways," Clint drawled and smiled, pleased at her concern for him. "I made it through the badlands and finally wound up in Sundown."

"All the way back into town? That was some ride!"

"I'd say it was. I left your buckskin in town at the livery and borrowed one of their horses to come home."

"I'll have Frank bring him home and take the stable horse back," Becky said and turned back to putting dishes on the table. "They never caught you, I guess?"

"No, but I made the mistake of going to the cafe and ran into Carl Farr and several of his men. They would have worked me over quite good if your friend Tim Harding hadn't stepped in."

"Tim!" Becky exclaimed.

"Yep. He took Farr's gun away from him and held it on him until the men left me alone. He stayed with me, bought my supper, and then rode through town with me just in case they tried anything else. He's a lot more man than I had given him credit for."

"I'll be danged!" Monte said in disbelief. "Tim Harding? The heck you say."

"Tim's a fine young man," Helen said from the stove. "His mama kept him home too much when he was growing up but he's a fine man. A lot like his dad in ways. Not the fire eater old Flint is but a good man."

"I told him I hoped he hadn't done himself any harm by helping me, and he just said the last thing Carl Farr wanted was to make his dad mad so he didn't seem to think they would bother him."

"He's right about that," Monte said. He rubbed his head as he spoke. "Old Flint Harding would tear Farr and his whole outfit up in little pieces if he hurt that boy. No, Tim's in no danger from Carl Farr."

"He also said to tell you he'd be out sometime today to give us a hand," Clint added.

"The hell you say!" Again Monte shook his head. "Don't know what we need with a home guard."

"Home guard or not, after what he did last night, I'd not mind having his help," Clint said and a twinkle came to his eyes. "Of course, he didn't mention helping you and me, Monte. I think it was Becky he meant to help."

Monte snorted and pulled at his mustache to hide the smile on his lips as he sat down at the table.

They made a short circle that day and made no attempt to push out the few head of Payne and Cameron cows they found. Shortly after they returned to the ranch, Tim Harding rode in on a good-looking black horse, leading a second one on which was tied his bedroll and war sack. Becky went to meet him.

"Clint told us you were coming out. Good to see you," she said, greeting him.

"I should have come long ago," Tim said, swinging down. "I'm afraid the Hardings haven't been the neighbors we should have been."

"It isn't your fight," Becky told him.

"No, but you're my special friend."

The next morning at breakfast Clint asked if Tim could ride with him.

"I want to pay this Smokey Bennett outfit a little visit," he explained. "I think I can persuade Smokey it will be bad for his health to keep trying to run any more of our stock. I might even be able to find the rest of your cows. I saw some of them when I was going through the badlands."

"I'm going with you!" Monte thundered. "We'll all go."

"No, I think it would be better if you and Becky kept an eye on things here," Clint said. "We may be gone a couple of days and someone ought to be watching for a push from our other neighbors."

Monte agreed reluctantly. Clint was right but it really galled the old man to think someone else was going to get to tell Smokey how he should behave. But he knew if he went, Becky would insist on going and he did not want to endanger the girl.

"You take care, Monte," Clint said evenly. "It's more likely you'll meet up with Emil Watson or Bud Jarvis than we will. Don't take any chances. We'll push their cows back after Tim and I get back."

"Don't worry about us," Becky said softly. "You be careful yourselves."

Monte assigned a few horses for Tim to ride and the young man caught one for that day. Clint caught the red roan that had been in Juan's string and was the horse Clint had seen Juan ride the first day he had been at the Major ranch. Shortly afterward, the two men rode from the ranch. The day was dark and gloomy and the rain continued to fall.

The men followed the trail Becky and Monte had used to return the cattle they found. Having never been there before, the men had to go from there somewhat by instinct. What seemed to be the right trail finally dropped off into a deep canyon that they thought had to be the one Monte described as being where Smokey Bennett's little spread was. The normally dry stream bed in the floor of the canyon was now running a little muddy water from the recent rain. They drew their horses to a stop at the edge of the trickle.

"Up or down?" Tim asked.

"I'm not sure," Clint acknowledged, rubbing his chin in thought. "I guess up the canyon. It looks like it might widen out up there a ways, maybe wide enough for a small ranch."

"Bennett has a few shirt-tail relatives living on some spreads scattered around the badlands," Tim told him. "They all have the reputation of stealing a few cows from the big ranches, but the only one who was ever caught was Smokey. He just got out of the pen a few months ago."

"That's what I understood Monte to say."

"Kind of funny he's so anxious to get back," Tim observed casually.

"I think he couldn't resist trying to get away with a few head, knowing we have our hands full trying to keep the other outfits off our grass. The one thing I can't figure is where would he sell this many? From what Monte said none of the Bennetts ever stole more than one or two at a time, mostly slick calves, old enough to wean but not branded. I'd guess we've had a couple hundred run off. There was darn near fifty in that bunch Monte found and brought back."

"Oh, I'd bet his relatives were all in on this with him," Tim said. "They may have split up what they stole and each one could hold his share until they had time to work the brands over and find a buyer who wouldn't ask too many questions."

"Still looks kind of organized to me for a fellow who had been used to a calf or two," Clint mused. "Maybe they've always had big dreams but never a chance before."

"Don't suppose the boys pushing in on the Majors was asking Smokey to make more room do you? Tim asked if he could keep you busy hunting your lost stuff, you'd not have time to run their stuff off."

"You know, Tim, you're almost half smart," Clint said and grinned. "You may just have hit it on the head. I've been running around in circles so much I'd never thought of that angle."

It was midafternoon when the two riders sloshed through the mud in front of Smokey's cabin. Clint motioned for Tim to stay well back and to one side. Tim unbuttoned his slicker to be able to get to his pistol, if needed.

Clint drew his horse to a stop at the hitching post and dismounted. While he tied the horse to the ring at the top of the post, his eyes swept the building and surrounding trees and corrals for any sign of life. The rain had stopped, at least temporarily. The only sound he heard was water dripping from the eaves of the house and from the trees. The scent of wet cedars and piñons was sweet to his nostrils and covered up any other odors.

Not wanting to give the impression of anything but strength, Clint walked boldly to the house and noisily ascended the creaking steps. He pounded loudly on the door. There was no answer.

"Anyone home!" he called.

He again called loudly and banged on the door.

"I'll go inside and leave a message," he said loudly. "I sure want Smokey to know we've been here and we're on to what he has been doing."

Clint pushed the door open slowly to gaze in at the cluttered mess of the room. He kicked the door open wider to let in more light. Surely no one lived here under these conditions. He called loudly again but only silence answered. With his eyes searching every spot in the room, he moved across, picking his way carefully over and around the scattered items. Droplets of rainwater rolled from his slicker to the floor.

He searched the house and found no one. The bedroom was not as messed up as the front room, but it was plain that someone had taken most of the clothing from the drawers and closet cupboard with its doors hanging open. After a brief look around, he returned through the clutter of the front room to the door.

"Looks like somebody already wrecked this joint," he called to his restless and watchful companion. "I don't know if it was someone else after Bennett or what. There's no sign of anyone here. Do you have anything to write with? I'd like to leave a message in case Bennett comes back."

"I always carry a pencil," Tim drawled, his dark eyes never stopping their watchfulness. He fished in his shirt pocket for the stub pencil he carried. He rode close to the house as Clint came to get it.

Back inside, Clint found a piece of cardboard and printed a message. He did not want its receiver to make any mistake. Clint left the message propped prominently on top of the old sofa.

Back outside, Clint swung into his saddle and felt the dampness of the seat—the drizzle had started again. It was time they should be heading back toward the ranch, but he hated not to leave his message in person with some of the Bennett clan.

"I never came close to this canyon when I was circling this rough country day before yesterday," he said softly. "I stayed south of here all the way. A few months ago, I crossed it a lot farther down country. I wonder if Bennett's relatives live in this canyon or somewhere else."

"The road should lead us someplace," Tim spoke up. "I wonder where it drops off into this canyon?"

They moved away from the buildings and empty corrals, following the track of the wagon road, which led up the canyon. After about a mile, the road left the canyon floor and wound its way up the steep side. A well-traveled trail broke away from the road and led on up the canyon. The riders drew up here for a moment. The rain had stopped and the sky was clearing, so they dismounted and slipped out of the yellow slickers.

"It'll be dark in a couple of hours," Tim said. "You want to keep going away from home?"

"Let's take the trail up the canyon a ways," Clint suggested. "If we don't find anything in an hour, we'll head back."

Without a word, his companion swung his horse behind Clint's and followed him up the trail, which followed along the twisting canyon for some time. At last they came to a large opening in the canyon where the hillsides were not nearly as steep and several branch draws came together. Here there were some good grass-covered flats and they found cattle grazing peacefully. Riding through these cattle, Clint found several carrying the Major brand. There was no sign any attempt had been made to change any of the brands. There were other cattle here, too, mostly a scrubby bunch that looked as though they had been inbred for years. These cattle all carried a brand Clint had never seen before.

At the upper end of the large basin, around the bend of one of the side canyons, they found a cabin, corrals, and sheds. Several thin horses stood in the corrals and smoke came from the black stovepipe that was anchored to the roof of the cabin by several guy wires. The cabin and corrals had the same unkempt, run-down appearance of Smokey's place.

Without a word, the two riders again spread out, with Tim falling behind and to Clint's side. Clint pulled the roan up before the cabin and shifted his weight in the saddle to be in a good position to grab his rifle should he need it.

"Hello the house!" he called loudly.

Immediately, there came the sounds of chairs scraping across the floor, one apparently crashed over backward in someone's haste to move. A dog suddenly barked viciously and came running around the corner of the house and the roan whirled and snorted excitedly. Clint pulled the horse up and forced him to swing back to face the dog, which was now snarling as it came stiff-legged toward the roan. Clint knew instantly the roan was not used to dogs. If that dog kept coming at the horse, Clint was going to be in serious trouble. A fleeting thought came to his mind of how silly he would look if he got himself thrown.

"Hello!" he called again. "Call off your dog!"

The dog stopped, still growling fiercely. When no one came to the door, the dog again began advancing and Clint quickly loosened his lariat. He shook out a loop and got ready to swing it at the dog if it came any closer.

"Call off your dog before I beat the hell out of him!" he called again. "I want to talk to you!"

The dog suddenly darted forward and leaped for the roan's shoulder, his teeth flashing. Clint swung the doubled rope with all his might. The rope connected with a dull thud and an immediate yelp of pain came from the startled animal. The roan whirled and began to buck when Clint tried to hold him from bolting. The horse made two high, vicious pitches, but Clint managed to hang on by dropping the rope and grabbing the saddle horn. This was no time to make any fancy rides. After those first few pitches, Clint managed to pull the horse up and swing him back toward the cabin. He put spurs to the roan's sides and the horse humped stiff-legged but moved a little closer to the cabin as the door was finally flung open.

There was no light inside and Clint could not make out any figure near the door. Already, the descending sun was sending long shadows across the canyon floor. Dusk was not far away.

"Is Smokey Bennett here?" Clint demanded, trying to keep his eyes on the door and the dog at the same time. If the dog attacked again he would be in a tight spot without his rope. He did not want to shoot the dog if he could possibly avoid it.

Finally a man's voice called from the cabin. "Who the hell wants to know?"

"I do," Clint snapped back. "We're the Major outfit."

"Smokey ain't here."

"How about any of his relatives?"

"Not here."

"What's your name?"

"Smith."

"Well, Mr. Smith, how about calling off your dog and letting us come in for a talk?" Clint asked.

"What about?"

"The Major cows we just seen in your pasture."

There was some hesitation while a whispered conversation was carried on by those inside the cabin. Clint could hear people moving about and he tensed in his saddle, ready to grab his rifle and throw himself off the horse at the first sign of trouble. The dog was showing signs of recovering from his first setback and acted as though he was about to gather enough courage for another attack. The roan could also sense the dog's feelings and moved nervously, again ready to whirl and bolt from that part of the country.

"Well, what about it?"

"Hold your horses," the voice called. "We're thinking on it."

"You hold that dog!" Clint warned.

"All right, all right! Rattler, get back under the house, you dumb mutt! How come you didn't warn us these jaspers were coming, anyway?"

The dog made no move to go back under the house but it did seem to have lost its intent for another charge. A man now appeared at the door of the cabin and spoke sharply to the dog. The animal slunk away.

Clint held his horse as he swung down. He led the horse to where his rope lay and stooped down to pick it up. He took his time coiling the rope neatly and hanging it back on the saddle before leading the horse to the steps of the cabin. The man in the doorway appeared unarmed but Clint could hear others inside, and from the sounds they were hurrying about, moving or hiding something. There was too much noise for normal activity.

"Mr. Smith, we seen quite a few Major cows along the big

draw we just rode through," Clint now said coldly. "You know how they got there?"

The man in the door, short and squat, spat tobacco juice a few feet from Clint. The man's squinty eyes drifted from Clint to the mounted man who now rode a little closer.

"Just drifted in," the man said through full lips. His appearance was as unkempt as the rest of the place.

"Sure funny," Clint mused as though just thinking out loud. "Those cattle are all new to this country. You wouldn't think they would leave the herd they were used to being with and drift way over here."

"Oh, I saw cows do lots of strange things," the man replied. "You can never tell what an old cow will do."

"Well, I'd like to take them home," Clint said. "However, it's too late to start tonight."

"Guess you'll have to come back some other time, then."

"I think maybe we had just better spend the night with you and take them back in the morning," Clint said, his keen eyes on the other man's face, but his ears were catching another flurry of sounds from inside the house. "Like you said, you never know what an old cow will do, and these might decide to drift on out of here just like they drifted in."

The man glanced over his shoulder into the house. When he turned back he again spat tobacco juice a short distance from Clint's foot.

"Suit yourself," he grunted. "You can put your horses in one of the corrals. We ain't got much food prepared but you're welcome."

"Thanks, Mr. Smith. We'll just do that."

Clint removed his rifle from the saddle boot, and Tim rode up to take the reins of the roan to lead him to the corrals. Clint walked up the steps to the shack, carrying the rifle loosely in his right hand. The squat rancher stepped back and Clint followed him inside.

It took a moment for his eyes to grow accustomed to the dimness of the room. Two young men stood at the stove at the far end of the cabin. One appeared to be trying to repair the hook on the screen of a high window. Clint's quick eye caught four plates on the table and guessed someone had crawled out that window—the cause of the noise while they had been talking. The two at the table were young men in their early twenties and Clint guessed them to be the squat rancher's sons.

"Sure appreciate your hospitality, Mr. Smith," Clint said easily and stood the rifle in the corner by the door. "My name's Austin and I ride for the Majors."

"So you said."

"These your boys, Mr. Smith?"

"Yeah," the squat rancher replied, not offering to introduce them.

"Don't know where we might find Smokey Bennett, do you? We want to see him kinda bad."

"His place is a few miles down the canyon," the man commented noncommittally.

"We know where his place is," Clint said and smiled thinly. "Looked like someone had ransacked it when we was there this afternoon. No sign of your friend Smokey, though."

"What you looking for Smokey for?" the older boy asked. It was then he remembered the fourth plate and moved to where he thought he hid it from Clint's view.

"Why, I'm sure he knows who's been helping our cows drift in this direction," Clint drawled in that soft southern tone he sometimes used. "We picked up quite a bunch of our cattle over close to his place a couple of days ago. They hadn't drifted there—we followed the tracks of several riders pushing them."

The squat rancher shrugged his shoulders and walked to the kitchen range.

"My partner is a pretty good tracker," Clint continued in his soft drawl. "He'll be on the lookout for the horses that made those tracks." He thought he could detect a tightening of the faces of the two young men but could detect nothing from Mr. Smith's back. "We know Smokey was one of the riders but we don't know who the others were. We ain't real sure just why they would drift all those cattle away from our place, but we aim to see that it's stopped."

Again the squat rancher shrugged and put all his attention to building up a fire in the stove.

"Set two more places," he spoke roughly to the boys. "We'll just have to make do with what we've got."

The younger boy immediately began rattling dishes in the cupboard, and the older boy kept himself between the dishes that were on the table and Clint.

"If you should see Smokey anytime, I'd sure take it a personal favor if you was to tell him we know what he's been up to and that Harvey Major is going to call on him in a few days. Harvey always likes to know how his ex-prisoners are getting along," Clint went on even though the three were making great efforts not to appear interested in what he was saying. "Harvey takes a lot of interest in seeing a man stays straight after he gets out of the pen."

"I'm sure he does," Mr. Smith said sourly.

A few minutes later, Tim stomped up the steps making a great deal of noise by scraping the mud from his boots. The dog growled from the corner of the house but kept his distance. The man who called himself Smith went to open the door for his uninvited guest.

The two young men put the meal of fried venison and potatoes on the table and the guests ate heartily and in silence. When it was finished, Mr. Smith lit his second coal-oil lamp and led the way into the back room, which held an iron double bedstead.

"You'll have to double up," he said and seemed to apologize. "This is all the beds we've got."

"Oh, this is fine, Mr. Smith," Clint assured the man. "I'll tell you we won't forget this."

The sandy-haired cowboy followed his host back into the

main living room. As the squat rancher watched solemnly, Clint went to the corner by the door and picked up his rifle.

"Kind of like to keep this by my bed," he said and smiled thinly, his hard blue eyes looking squarely at the Smiths. "I'm kind of a light sleeper."

"I figured that already," Mr. Smith said sarcastically as he turned away.

"I'll just leave the bedroom door open, too," Clint added. "See you in the morning."

He walked back into the bedroom where his companion was now stretched out on the bed.

Tim was fully clothed except for his boots. He watched Clint silently for any sign or signal. Clint winked at him and worked the action of the Winchester, putting a cartridge in the chamber. Tim knew the sound would carry to the Smiths in the other room. Clint eased the hammer to half cock and laid the rifle on the bed.

"Like to keep one in the chamber at night," he said in a loud whisper. "Never know when you might have to get off a quick shot."

"I like a pistol better," Tim drawled in reply.

Clint then lowered his voice to a whisper only Tim could hear. "You sleep and I'll stay awake for a while, just in case."

Tim nodded in understanding and Clint blew out the lamp. The only sound they heard during the night was the horses stirring in the corrals. At least a portion of this could be natural, caused by their horses being strange to those of the Smiths. Even though in separate corrals, they snorted, whinnied, and occasionally kicked at each other, usually striking the pole fence.

Morning came with considerable chill in the air. Fall was not far away. Clint threw back the blanket he had pulled over him and rolled off the bed. His companion eyed him silently and then followed his example. They made sure their hosts would hear them stirring about. Tim took particular delight in stomping into his boots as loudly as he could, a big grin breaking across his face.

Clint carried his rifle with him as he went into the main room of the cabin. Mr. Smith and one of the boys stood at the kitchen range laying a fire. The second boy stood in the doorway of the back room, his hand rumpling his hair. They all looked sleepily at their guests.

"Tim, let's go check the horses," Clint said evenly. "They sure fussed most of the night."

Without a word, Tim turned to follow him out the door. They did not speak until they were at the corrals and out of earshot of the house.

"How many horses were in that corral last night?" Clint asked and leaned against the pole gate.

"Four."

"Only three there now."

"Sure enough. The missing one is a bald-faced black, branded LB. These three are all Box N."

"I thought I heard someone in the corrals last night," Clint said, his suspicions pretty well confirmed. "I'm sure someone went out that back window while Mr. Smith was talking to me at the door when we first rode up. He was stalling me, and I'll bet anything Smokey Bennett went out that window and hid until we was in bed. Then he caught his horse and lit out."

"He's scared," Tim said.

"He got the message I wanted to deliver, anyway."

They caught their horses and saddled them before returning to the house.

"That roan thinks his throat has been cut," Clint remarked as they shut the gate behind them. "He's sure not used to working two days in a row with nothing to eat in between. It's an experience he's never had before."

"Won't hurt him none," Tim drawled. "I've had to do the same thing and it only stunted me a little."

"Well, let's see if Mr. Smith has our breakfast ready."

"Mr. Smith. Wonder what his real name is."

"I'll bet you anything it's Bennett."

As they walked back to the cabin, Clint wondered what Becky and Monte were doing this morning. He couldn't help but worry about them meeting up with some of the neighbors without his being there to handle things.

CHAPTER 13

AFTER Clint and Tim had ridden away, Becky and Monte rode through the rain, both hunched over in their slickers.

"This moisture should really make some good fall and winter feed," Becky said, trying to think of something cheery and positive to say. It was fairly warm and pleasant in spite of the drizzle.

"If we only had our own cows to feed in place of all our neighbors', this old country would winter them in fine shape," Monte said, his eyes taking note of the condition of the range as they rode. "If things had only worked out as Vance had planned. With the market up like it is, we could sell the steers for almost enough to pay Farr off and keep all the calves over for next year."

"I can't help but wonder," Becky commented, "if somebody is deliberately pushing in on us just to make it impossible for us to pay that note. I suppose Russ and Sid could be just trying to expand, maybe Farr, too. But Farr's men sure tried to keep us from finding those cattle yesterday, and that makes you think they either moved our cows themselves or they know who did."

"Yeah, maybe old Farr even encouraged someone to steal our cattle and then they would feel they had to cover for him." Monte's faded eyes peered through the drizzle at the woman beside him. "I sure hope those boys don't take on more trouble than they can handle. A whole bunch of Bennetts can be pretty tough customers."

"I do wish they had waited for Harvey," Becky added. "Even if Farr is behind this, Harvey wouldn't hesitate to put the Bennetts where they belong. In fact, if we could only prove Farr is doing this to keep us from paying our note, Harvey would whip him within an inch of his life, father-in-law or not."

The old cowman turned his head slowly and looked at the woman, then turned away, saying nothing.

She was surprised. Could it be that Monte did not believe Harvey would stand up to his wife's father? Surely Monte could not think that. After all, both of the Major boys had grown into manhood under Monte's eye and guiding hand. He had brought them up better than that.

They found only a few strays between the ranch and the Big Spring, not enough to bother with. The weather lifted a short time and then the clouds lowered and the drizzle began again. The ground was saturated now and the horses slipped and sloshed through the mud with each step they took.

It was past noon when Monte suggested they return home by way of the Old Ranch.

"Looks like we're in luck today," he said as he turned his horse into the driving rain. "I guess them Farr boys don't like to punch cows in the rain any more than we do. Don't seem likely we'll find any cows in on us today."

"I hope it rains like this for weeks then," Becky said.

They rode across the muddy prairie for miles. Some of the draws were running several inches of water. They came to the main creek near the Old Ranch not far from where Susan's horse had fallen in the arroyo. By now the creek was up and had the most water it had held for years.

"I doubt we will find anything across the creek," Becky said, stopping her horse on the bank. "We've never had anything pushed in south of here."

"I'd feel a little better if we looked, anyway," Monte said. "You never know when they'll try something different and we haven't ridden that country in a spell."

"All right, but I'd just as soon go home."

"It won't take long to make a little circle on the way back to the ranch," the old cowboy said and eased his horse down the slick bank into the creek bed.

Becky's horse followed, sliding spraddle legged down the bank. They crossed the water now almost to the horses' bellies. The far bank was so slick Monte's horse almost fell twice before he finally reached the top.

"Ride up creek a little ways, Becky," Monte called down to her. "There's a better place to climb out up above here."

Becky followed his instructions and her horse made it to the top with no mishaps. They rode southwest into a part of the country they normally held for winter range. It was more broken, with rolling hills covered with cedars and piñon pine. They covered a good part of the area and began circling to the south back toward the ranch and horse pasture. They were moving along the edge of one of the cedar hills when they rounded a knob and found cattle. Twenty head or more moved away from them and more were coming around the next point of the little hill.

Monte cursed and lifted his horse into a trot, the animal sliding with each step. As the old cowboy rounded the little point, he suddenly shouted loudly and spurred his horse to a faster pace. Becky rose in her stirrups and spurred her horse to an unwilling trot. She rounded the point to see Monte's horse loping and sliding across the open country toward three men with a large group of cattle. Monte was waving his arm and yelling at them and she forced her horse into a lope, hoping to catch up with the old cowboy before he reached the men.

As she rode, she recognized Emil Watson, Cameron, and Payne. She could read the brands, too. The cattle were Farr's.

Then it happened. It seemed unbelievable, impossible. She saw the smoke first as it lifted from Watson's pistol. Then she heard the cracking sound of the shot. One shot. Monte's horse staggered to a stop and the old cowboy tumbled from his saddle to the mud, the horse jerking away to one side but turning to stop and stare down at the yellow slicker on the ground.

Becky's spurs sank home and her horse grunted loudly as it labored ahead. She saw the three men turn their horses and spur away from her. They looked back over their shoulders and whipped their mounts into a run, mud flying into the air from the animals' hind feet.

Becky slid her horse to a stop and swung down. Her horse was frightened at the yellow slicker on the ground and did not want to be led close, but she pulled furiously on the reins, her fear and her voice spooking the animal even more. Monte lay face down in the mud, not moving. She rolled him over, his old faded eyes looking sightlessly into the sky as the drizzle washed mud from his face.

Furiously she tore open the slicker and his blood-covered shirt. A bluish hole was centered in his chest. As she moved him, she could see blood and flesh of a much larger hole where the .45 slug had torn out his back and side.

"Oh, my God! It can't be!" she cried softly. "It can't be!"

She hugged Monte's face to her breast as she tried to plug the terrible hole with his shirt. Her hat tumbled into the mud and lay unnoticed.

How long she knelt there with the old man's head in her lap she did not know. Rain soaked her blonde hair and dripped from her nose and chin, mingled with her tears.

At last, she laid him gently back down, placing her hat beneath his white head. She took off her slicker and covered his head with it. She could not lift his lifeless body on his horse. All she could do was go to the ranch for help. She caught Monte's horse, then mounted her own.

It was really up to her, now. How she wished Clint or Harvey or Vance were there. She tried to force herself to think as one of them would have. She went through the horse pasture and gathered the horses, driving them to the corrals at the ranch.

At her news, Helen almost went into hysterics.

"What will we do!" the woman exclaimed. "We must get Harvey. We must get Harvey!"

"First, we've got to bring Monte home," Becky said, trying to hold her voice steady to calm the other. "You bundle up the children—we can't leave them—and I'll get on some dry clothes and harness the team."

"Are you sure it was Watson?" Helen asked, hurrying to get herself and the youngsters ready.

"Yes, I'm sure. I saw him and I saw his gun. I saw him do it and then all three turned and ran."

"Did Monte shoot at them?"

"No, he never had his gun out. His slicker was buttoned and he couldn't have gotten it out if he had tried. I am sure it was still in his holster . . . but I admit I didn't look."

They hurried. Becky changed into dry range clothes and found her brother's old slicker. It was much too large for her and she rolled up the sleeves so she could put her hands out. She quickly caught and harnessed the team and hitched them to the wagon. Changing her mind, she unhooked them and rehitched them to the buggy. Its box would be big enough to carry Monte, and the lighter vehicle wouldn't sink in the mud so badly. Also, the top would give the people inside some protection from the rain.

She drove to the house, where Helen hurried the youngsters out and into the buggy.

"I forgot. We should have some blankets," Helen said and hurried back into the house, throwing her hands wildly into the air as she walked. She was back shortly, breathing heavily, and labored as she climbed into the buggy with two wool blankets. The seat was crowded but the two children knew better than to complain. Susan sat on Helen's lap with Little Harvey between the women. They whispered between themselves but did not speak loudly enough for the women to hear.

There was no road, and Becky had to drive around many gullies to find places they could cross. The team was willing but their footing was so poor they often almost fell in the slippery muck. It took over an hour to reach the yellow slickers covering Monte's body. The team snorted and one horse almost went down as they tried to back away from the strange object. Becky finally got them close and stopped the team.

It was as she was dismounting she noticed Monte's right hand, now pointing up over his head. The man lay face down—not as she had left him. Could it be the old man was still alive? She lifted the slicker over his head, but his face held the same fixed expression it had when she left.

There was his pistol now a few inches from his right hand. It had not been that way! For a few moments she stood there staring down, not able to believe her eyes. What was going on? Why?

"Don't come near, Helen!" she shouted. "Someone's been here!"

There were tracks, bigger than hers. Deep tracks, blotched by the rain but still there. Someone much heavier than she had been there. She bent over and picked up the gun, flipping the loading gate to see the empty hole where Monte would have carried the gun with the hammer on that empty. She rolled the cylinder enough to see the dent in the cap on the next shell. One shot had been fired.

"Someone came back after I left," she said to Helen. "They took his gun out and fired one shot." She stood looking up at her sister still in the buggy.

"You mean it wasn't like that before?"

"It certainly was not. You can see where my knees were. I knelt there for some time holding Monte's head in my lap. I had rolled him over on his back and his arm was not up like that. I'm sure his gun was in the holster. See, I tore his slicker getting it open."

"Is it possible he was alive and moved after you left?"

"Oh, I don't think so. I'm sure he could not have moved like that. Watson or one of them must have come back after

I left to make sure he was dead. Must have fired one shot from his gun so they can claim Monte fired at them first. I know those deeper marks were not here and I did not make them."

Becky got back into the buggy and managed to maneuver the team close to the slicker on the ground. She handed the reins to Little Harvey as she and Helen climbed down. The two women struggled in the mud to get Monte's body into the back of the buggy, where they covered him with the blankets and slickers, before climbing aboard. Becky took the reins from the little boy's hands.

"If it happened like you said, it was definitely murder," Helen said determinedly. "Harvey will make Watson pay for that."

"We'll have to take Monte to town and get Harvey," Becky admitted. "I hope he can arrest Watson on my testimony. Even Harvey can't just do anything without evidence. He has to follow the law. And, I'll have to tell the truth about how we found him this time with his gun out and a shot fired. It will just be my word against the three of them."

"You saw it," Little Harvey spoke up. "That ought to be enough evidence for anybody."

"Maybe Harvey can get Russ or Sid to tell the truth, too," Helen suggested as they started for the long drive home.

"From the hold Farr seems to have on them, I'd not bank on it. If it comes to court, you can bet your bottom dollar I'll be the one that has to testify against Watson, and they'll all three claim self-defense and that Monte shot first."

"From all the stories about Watson and his brothers, I'd not put it past them to try something to shut you up," Helen continued bluntly. "You'll be in more danger than anyone if he thinks you can send him to the pen."

"I only hope Clint and Tim are back when we get to the ranch," Becky said as dusk settled over the land and they neared the horse pasture fence. Once through the gate they could at least be on a trail.

"Let's hope they didn't run into trouble with some of the Bennetts," Helen added, worry plain in her voice. "They didn't even think they would be back tonight."

"They probably won't. We've got to take Monte to town and get Harvey," Becky said firmly. "Then I'll have to come back and find them."

Both women's hearts were heavy with sadness as they drove through the dusk toward the ranch. The buggy wheels made sucking noises as they cut through the mud and the horses slipped with each step they took. Occasionally mud from their feet would fly up into the faces of the four in the buggy but they paid little attention.

Becky's mind drifted between her thoughts of Monte and all he had meant to her family and wondering where Clint was and if he was in danger. She was torn between feeling she should take Monte's body to town and wanting to find Clint.

CHAPTER 14

BREAKFAST was eaten in the same sullen silence as the evening meal. As soon as they finished, Clint pushed back his chair and stood up.

"Much obliged for the accommodations, Mr. Smith," he drawled easily. "We'll gather our cows and head for home."

The squat rancher scraped his chair across the floor and sat away from the table for a moment. He kept his hands flat on the top of the table. "Get our horses saddled, boys," he growled out of the side of his mouth. "We'll help these men gather their stuff. I'll be darn glad to be rid of those cows."

"I'll just bet you will," Tim said and laughed softly. "A few extra cows can sure eat up a fellow's grass."

It took them most of the morning to ride the canyons and gather all of the Major cattle they could find—about thirty pairs of cows with calves and about twenty steers. After these had been separated from Smith's cattle they were pushed against one side of the canyon.

"What's the best trail to take them back to the Major outfit?" Clint asked his host casually as they were about to part company.

"There's a good trail takes off up the next fork in the canyon. It will bring you out on top, west of the Majors' Big Spring pasture. Once you get out, just work east about five or six miles and you'll hit Payne's fence. There's a trail through Payne's pasture that will take you right to the Major place."

"I know the trail you're talking about," Clint nodded. "Well, so long, Mr. Smith."

"Yeah."

The squat rancher reined his horse around and his boys moved to flank him. He spat a large stream of wet black tobacco juice.

"Oh, Mr. Smith," Clint added. "Next time you see Smokey riding that bald-faced black LB horse, you tell him we're sorry we missed him. But, I'm sure Harvey Major will be out to see him real soon."

The three Smiths acted as though they had not heard him, turned their horses and lifted them to a trot, apparently heading back for their ranch.

"They'll get the word to Smokey, don't you worry," Tim commented and moved his horse to turn their cows down the canyon. "A few more weeks and I'll bet these calves, at least, would have been wearing a different brand."

Late afternoon found the two riders pushing the cows and their weary calves through the gate between the Payne pasture and Major land. It was then Clint noticed the rider loping toward them from the direction of the Big Spring. He realized instantly it was Becky Major, not that he could make out her features from that distance, but he recognized the way the rider sat her horse.

"Push those cows away from the fence, Tim," Clint called. "I'll go report to the boss lady."

Clint lifted the roan to a long easy lope and swiftly cut the distance between himself and Becky. As they grew closer, he could make out the expression on the woman's face and he knew something had happened.

They both pulled their horses to a trot and closed the last twenty feet between them.

"What's happened, Becky?" he asked as their horses half-passed and stopped with the riders facing each other.

"It's Monte." Her voice was shaking with emotion. "Watson killed him!"

With this, the tears she had been holding back began to flow and almost before he knew what happened, his arms went around her and she nestled her head against his shoulder. For a few moments she sobbed softly with her face turned away from him. In spite of the circumstances, he was conscious of the thrill going through his body at her touch. The roan moved slightly, being unused to two riders acting in this manner and he was jerked rather roughly to a stand.

"Thank God you're back safely," she whispered at last. "When you didn't come home last night, I began to imagine all kinds of things."

Their horses moved and he had to release his hold on her. In spite of himself, Clint silently cussed the roan horse.

"How did it happen, Becky?" he asked.

She now seemed more in control of herself and sat back in her saddle. She spoke clearly, determined to get it out.

"We caught Payne, Cameron, and Watson pushing Farr cows in on us southwest of the Old Ranch. Monte went for the men, shouting at them to come get the cows and cussing them as only he could. Watson shot him right out of the saddle. Monte never had a chance. Didn't have his gun out. I started toward Monte, and the three of them took out as fast as their horses could run." The woman's eyes dropped to the ground. "Monte was dead when I got to him."

"I hoped it wouldn't come to this," the man said slowly as the real shock of what had happened began to reach his mind. "Monte was the finest."

"That's not all, either, Clint. When Helen and I went to get Monte in the buggy, Watson or someone had come back, taken Monte's gun out of the holster, and fired one shot from it. They had rolled Monte over on his stomach, raised his right arm over his head, and left the pistol a few inches from his hand."

"The hell you say!"

"You know they will claim Watson killed him in self-defense. I'm sure they came back and did that hoping whoever came for the body would have to testify Monte had his gun out and had fired one shot. They probably didn't think I'd come back for him without some of you men."

"I'm sure you're right, Becky," Clint said slowly, watching every expression on the woman's face. "That was pretty clever of them. They know your brother will have to take it to court and they know Carl Farr can probably buy the judge and plenty of witnesses, if not your brother."

"I doubt Harvey will even be able to bring Watson to trial," she said bitterly. "How I hate that man. He's killed one of the best men who ever walked and will probably get away with it."

"Oh, maybe not. Where's your brother? I'm surprised he let you come here alone."

"Harvey's still in Santa Fe. We left word for him to come and sent Vance a telegram, too."

"Well, let's get back to the ranch," Clint said softly. He turned in his saddle and waved to where Tim was still driving the cattle. "Let's go, Tim!" he called loudly. "We've got trouble!"

Harvey was not at the ranch when they arrived but Frank and Helen were there, having come from town to help Becky get ready for Monte's funeral. Becky left Clint and Tim at the corrals and hurried to the house.

Frank said that Harvey should be in on the train that night but it would take Vance several days to get there—perhaps not in time for the funeral. He and Helen had set the funeral for Monte on Saturday, just three days away.

Clint ran the horse herd into the corrals and put two horses in one of the small pens before he went to the house. He had also put one of Becky's horses and the team for the spring wagon in another corral and fed them all hay.

Helen had a supper waiting. Susan sat beside Clint, as she had developed a great fondness for the tall rider ever since the episode with the snake. The cowboy put his arm around her shoulders, knowing old Monte had meant a lot to both of these children. Little Harvey came to sit on the other side of Clint. Across the table, Tim sat by Becky who barely picked at her food, her mind on Monte.

Clint liked Tim. Home guard or not, he had done his part at the Bennetts' and Clint was glad he was there. At the same time, he could not help being a little jealous of the way Tim felt so free around Becky. He realized they had been friends for a long time but he resented their closeness. The memory of her touch when they had met this afternoon was still strong and kept crowding into his thoughts.

As Clint lit his pipe after the meal, Frank suddenly looked across the table at the cowboy. "By golly, Clint," he exclaimed, "I almost forgot. I brought a letter for you. What did you do with it, Helen?"

"I think I put it on a shelf in the cupboard." Helen got up and reached under a platter on the second shelf for the envelope. "How did your girlfriend find out where you were, Clint?" she asked in a teasing manner. "It's sure a woman's handwriting but no return address."

"Must have tracked me down," Clint said, reaching for the envelope.

He used a table knife to slit open the envelope and take out a single sheet of paper. He read it carefully. When he had finished he looked across at Becky.

"Good news, I hope," she said, her dark eyes searching his face amiably. She was more than a little curious for she, too, remembered their meeting and she had seen enough to know it was indeed a woman's writing.

In response to her question he merely handed the sheet of paper to her. She unfolded it and read aloud.

" 'Dear Pecos' . . . Who is Pecos?" she asked, looking up at him.

"My friends on the Arrowhead Ranch call me that," he answered, looking only at Becky. "I remember the first morning I was here, Monte asked about my gray having the Arrowhead brand and I told him I bought the horse from a trader in Raton. I think that's the only lie I ever told him. However, I do have a bill of sale from a trader in Raton."

Becky read on, " 'Good to know where you are. I must say

you write almost as much as you talk. Clay has been very anxious to get word to you. The governor has agreed to give you a complete pardon, as long as you haven't been in any more shootings, unless as a duly elected or appointed peace officer. The governor understands you were on your way to get deputized by the sheriff when you shot that man. So, we hope you managed to stay out of trouble. If you have, you can come home anytime. Ellen.' "

Again Becky's eyes went to Clint's face.

"Ellen is Clay Hamilton's wife," he explained slowly. "They are the best friends I ever had. They own Arrowhead Ranch—I rode for that outfit ever since I drifted in there when Clay and I were both just kids." He was silent a moment, his eyes searching Becky's face. At last, he continued.

"I shot a man," Clint said, his eyes only on Becky. "Huerfano County has a lot of coal mines and there was a strike with some violence. The sheriff sent word there was going to be a run on the jail and he needed help. He had arrested some of the big trouble makers and he thought a mob was going to try to break them out."

Slowly, Clint told them his story. "I was alone at Arrowhead when the word came, so I left a note for Clay and rode into town. I never got to the sheriff's office and was never sworn in or got a badge. I had just gotten to town when I saw a group of miners giving old Judge Clayton a bad time. The judge—an old man in his seventies—was a dear friend and a part owner of Arrowhead Ranch. The miners thought he was against them and they all knew he was very close to the governor. They had the judge backed up against a store front and were threatening to beat him if he didn't get the governor to come to Walsenburg and force the sheriff to release their leaders."

Clint paused a moment.

"I'll bet you jumped right into them," Susan said softly, her eyes shining brightly.

"Well, I do some foolish things at times," Clint admitted, looking down at her and then returning his eyes to Becky's face as he continued his story.

Clint had pushed his way to Judge Clayton and advised them to keep back and leave the judge alone. He saw one man go for a gun, and Clint shot him. One of the others picked up the man's gun and hid it under his coat and began shouting Clint had killed an unarmed man, but they did back off enough for Clint to push the judge to safety inside a store. Clint grabbed his horse and ran. Some of the men got horses and came after him, but they couldn't catch him.

He met Clay and the other Arrowhead men riding for town and told them what had happened. His horse was winded, and Clay had insisted on swapping horses with him, the gray he rode into the Major ranch.

Clint had hidden out in a line cabin until Clay got word to him to get out of state because things were such he couldn't get a fair trial and Clay was afraid the miners would lynch him if he turned himself in. Clay said he'd get to the governor and that Clint should let him know where he could reach him after things got settled. He concluded, "As you can see, Clay did what he said he would."

He again paused a moment.

"To tell the truth, this will be the second pardon Clay got for me," he said, his eyes lowered to look at the table. "When I first rode into the Arrowhead I was just a kid of fourteen and on the run for killing a man in Texas where I grew up— a man who had raped my mother. Clay was about my age, a couple years older, and we became friends. He persuaded the ranch owner to get the governor of Colorado to convince the governor of Texas to pardon me. So you can see why I think so much of him. I owe him a lot. I had a horse trader I knew in Raton give me a bill of sale for the Arrowhead horse I rode in here on."

"How did your friend know where to reach you?" Becky asked.

"When we were in town to get the cattle I mailed Clay a note that I was here at your ranch."

There was silence for a few minutes and Becky never let her eyes move from Clint's face.

"You've got to return to Colorado immediately," she said at length. "That pardon is the most important thing in the world to you."

"Oh, a few more days won't matter."

"It could. I know what you said about Watson. You think the law won't do anything to him, so maybe you plan on shooting him yourself."

Clint lowered his eyes and studied the tablecloth for a moment.

"That would be awful!" Helen exclaimed. "I'll admit he deserves to be shot but that wouldn't bring Monte back! It would only hurt you! Besides, Watson is a professional gunman."

"It would ruin your chance of getting that pardon, Clint," Becky added. "You get that idea right out of your head and ride out of here tomorrow for Colorado. I know now why you didn't want to get mixed up in our trouble."

He stood up, putting the letter back in the envelope. "Goodnight, all."

Clint was alone at the bunkhouse that night for some time because Tim stayed and visited with Becky and the Carlsons.

From the depths of his war sack, the cowboy brought out a pistol and belt, well protected by several layers of cloth. He cleaned and oiled the gun and put the shell belt around his hips. Leaving the cylinder empty, he holstered the gun. He cut a leather thong from an old bridle, put it through a hole in the bottom of the holster, and tied it around his leg. He made a draw. Handling a gun, any gun, had always been second nature to him.

"Darn slow," he mused bitterly. "I'll have to do a lot better than that."

He spent an hour practicing a pattern that had once been

a very familiar part of his daily life. He could not fire a shot because to do so would alarm the women, so he practiced and let the hammer fall on an empty chamber. Then he loaded the gun with five bullets and drew it several times to feel the added weight. He was not satisfied with his performance, but it would have to do.

The next morning, long before daylight, he rousted Tim from his bed. "I'm going to take a ride," he told the man softly. "If you want in on this, come on. I don't want to wake anyone at the house."

"Any chance I can talk you out of this?" Tim asked, all seriousness in his voice. "I say you should wait for Harvey. As Becky said, there's no reason to mess up your chance at a pardon."

"You coming?"

"Well, yes, then." Tim stuck his long, thin legs out from under the blankets.

The men dressed in the darkness and went to the corrals, where they caught the horses Clint had left up the night before.

They were careful to make as little noise as possible. They mounted their horses and rode away from the ranch at a slow walk, hoping no one at the house had heard them.

It was just sunup when they went through the gate onto Payne's property. Clint knew where Russ Payne's ranch was even though he had never been there.

Russ Payne and his two hired men had just come out of the house and were walking toward the corrals when Sid Cameron and his hired man rode into the ranch yard.

"You're sure on time, old buddy," Payne greeted his neighbor jovially. "We'll be with you as soon as we catch our horses."

"Two riders coming in from the east," Sid Cameron spoke, grumbling. "Anyone else supposed to be coming?"

"Not that I know of."

The rancher and his hands saddled their horses and mounted. They sat silently on their mounts, waiting for the riders to approach. Payne grunted slightly on recognizing Clint. Clint was riding the big bay horse Monte often had used and had been riding the day he was shot. Clint now rode the horse right up in front of the men while his companion stopped a short distance back and off to one side. Sid Cameron took in the hard look on their faces and was surprised at recognizing Tim Harding. The rancher's nervous eye was also quick to catch the pistol on Clint's hip, which he had never seen there before.

"You boys wouldn't happen to be heading for the Majors'?" Clint drawled, almost lazily.

"Just so happens we were." Russ Payne spat tobacco juice just in front of the bay horse.

"I had hoped you got my message to stay off Major range."

"We got cattle over there to look after," the rancher grunted. "It's open range and our cows got as much right there as anybody's."

"That's not the way we see it," Clint said. "Before we continue that discussion, do you know where I can find Watson?"

Payne shrugged his beefy shoulders with an expression indicating he did not know and cared less.

"Any of the rest of you know?"

Cameron's hired man looked at his employer but no one spoke.

"Well, it don't matter," Clint said. "I'll find him. Now, let's get back to you fellows. I understand Mr. Payne and Mr. Cameron, you were with Watson when he killed Monte. Either of you care to tell me about that?"

"Nothing to tell." Payne again spat tobacco juice and moved his quid to the other side of his jaw.

"Well, try to remember something. What story are you going to tell the sheriff?"

"Oh, I doubt Harvey will ask any questions of us," Payne

said, grinning crookedly and showing his tobacco-stained teeth. "Daddy Farr will explain it to him for us."

"Really?" Suddenly Clint's voice had a cutting edge. "Well, you tell me how it happened and do it quick. I ain't got no Daddy Farr."

"Well, old Monte come at us a-ridin' and yellin' and wavin' his pistol. Hell, Watson couldn't take a chance the old coot might hit one of us. We hollered at him to put the gun up and talk, but Monte just kept coming. Monte fired one shot. Watson waited as long as he dared and then shot in self-defense."

"You lie!" Clint said slowly, calmly. "Monte never had his gun out and you know it! Becky Major saw it happen and she said his gun was never out of his holster."

"Well, it might have looked that way to her," Payne said in an almost condescending tone. "She was off a ways behind Monte. She couldn't see his front. She really wasn't close enough to see good. We was right there with Monte a-comin' at us."

The roar of Clint's Colt took them all by surprise. The men quickly tried to pull in their reins to check the startled horses. They had not seen the cowboy's hand move but it now held a smoking, bone-handled .45. Russ Payne felt a tinge of pain in his right ear and something warm ran down the side of his neck and inside his shirt collar. Instinctively, his hand went up to his rather large ear. The bullet had cut a notch in the earlobe, which was bleeding freely. He was suddenly sick at his stomach and realized he had swallowed his tobacco.

"Who coached you how to tell it? Hal Flack or maybe even Carl Farr, himself? Well, I'll not believe you and I'll also settle with Watson as soon as I can find him. Now, Mr. Russ Payne, you are a marked man for life. Every time you see or feel that ear, it will remind you not to tell lies and not to try to run your cattle on range that ain't yours. You fellows all just sit tight, and my friend will relieve you of your shooting irons while I explain something to you." Clint kept the Colt loose in his hand and pointed in the general direction of the men as he spoke. "You ready to listen real good? I've got a suggestion for you fellows. You ride right on over to the Major place and gather all your stock and bring them back to your home range. The five of you should be able to get it done today if you work real hard. If I find one of your cows on Major range after today, I'm going to shoot the cow first and then you. You talked almighty big about having a right to that grass but if you want it you'll have to be able to whip us first."

"I suggest you listen to him real good," Tim spoke up, as he took their guns. "This man's known as Pecos up on the Arrowhead Ranch in Colorado. Besides, the Harding Ranch is also backing him. You aren't just fighting a woman and an old man anymore."

"We'll go get our cows," Cameron assured them hurriedly. "This has gone far enough. I never did like it, but we owed Farr so much money we had to do what he said. I sure don't want any more killing."

"We'll go get our cows," Payne said, holding his ear with blood still oozing out between his stubby fingers.

The five men lifted their reins and rode away from the corrals. Clint and Tim watched them go.

"What will we do with these extra guns?" Tim asked when the men were well out of earshot.

"Looks like a well there by the barn. Just drop them in that," Clint said. "You did right well, Tim."

"At least we got by that one without you killing anybody, Clint," Tim drawled. "You sure know how to handle that gun. Maybe we'll luck out."

"I hope so." There was no real conviction in Clint's voice. "Watson won't be so easy."

CHAPTER 15

CARL Farr had been aghast at the news Watson had actually killed Monte. Hal Flack had assured him the man would not use his gun except on explicit orders from the foreman.

"But hell, Carl," Flack said easily, "this finishes the Majors. That girl and Austin can't hold it alone. I'll send Watson out to one of the cow camps where he can hide out for a while and you tell your son-in-law sheriff it was self-defense. With Russ and Sid's word to back us, Harvey'll have to believe them. After all, what else can he do?"

"I'll talk to Harvey, all right, but you keep Watson right here at the ranch," the angry rancher snapped. "I want Harvey to think we're willing to turn him over if he has a case against him. We might even let Harvey arrest him to salve his conscience and then we can get him out later."

"I doubt that will work. Watson won't let Harvey arrest him."

"Well, Harvey can try," Farr said in open disgust. "You seem to forget I still hold some influence over him. Beth can handle him, too, if she has to. The main reason I made Harvey sheriff was to control the local law. I'm getting him that appointment as U.S. Marshal so we can move him out of here."

"All right. I'll keep Watson here—let's see what happens."

Watson was greatly surprised at the attitude of indifference Farr and the foreman showed him. He had expected to be fired and told to leave the country. Instead, Flack told him Farr would take care of the sheriff and he was to stay close to the ranch in case Austin showed up.

Bud Jarvis was also surprised at this attitude. He was even

more amazed that Watson stayed so calm after having killed a man. Bud had never thought it would come to this—he would beat a man with his fists but was in awe of a man killing another with a gun. Bud couldn't keep his eyes off the gunman as they sat on the porch of the bunkhouse, Watson in a straight-backed chair propped against the wall, his hat over his eyes as if taking a nap in the warm midmorning sun.

Becky did not sleep well that night. Her mind was troubled with thoughts of Monte, who had been like a second father to her. Clint was also on her mind. Finally she dropped off to sleep but fitfully dreamed about Monte, seeing him shot again. Then Clint was there with a pistol on each hip, facing Watson. Either way it came out, Clint would lose. She sat bolt upright in her bed trying to stop the duel. Her heart beat swiftly as she realized it had been a dream and she forced herself to lie back. It had seemed so real.

The sounds of horses moving around the corral came through her open window. She listened intently, trying to assure herself it was only the normal sounds of the horses being kept up at night. Major horses were unused to that. Was someone throwing a saddle on a horse's back? It couldn't be. Her dream must have caused her imagination to run away with her. It did sound as if one of the pole gates was being opened slowly—it had a way of making a little creak as it moved against the wooden gate post. Minutes later, one of the horses whinnied as though its partner had been taken away.

Wide awake now, she got up and dressed in her ranch clothes. She carried her boots outside and slipped into them where they would not make the noise they would have on the wooden floor.

She made her way to the corrals through the darkness. Her horse and the team were all that were left in one corral. Fear gripped her heart as she went into the barn. Clint's saddle, as well as Tim's, was missing. To make sure, she turned and ran to the bunkhouse where she knocked loudly, then went inside and lit the lamp. No one was there. She ran to the house and around the corner to the door of her room. Now, she made no pretense of being quiet. She knew Clint had gone to find Watson and her heart tightened in her chest. They had already lost Monte and now all she could think of was that they would lose Clint, too, just as her dream had foretold. No matter which way a duel ended, Clint would lose. He would lose his life or he would lose his pardon.

"Becky, what's happening?" Helen called. "Is something wrong?"

"There sure as hell is!" Becky snapped and settled the holstered .38 on her hip as Monte had taught her to do.

The door opened and Helen peered inside, carrying a lamp. Seeing her sister dressed, Helen came inside, clutching her long nightgown at her waist.

"What in the world? Never heard you swear before! What's happened?"

"Clint's gone. I'm sure he and Tim have gone to find Watson. They were sure careful not to wake us up so I could stop them or go with them." As she spoke, Becky piled her hair high on her head so she could put on her Stetson. "You wake Frank up while I saddle the horses. He'll have to ride to town and try to find Harvey or a deputy. Tell him to bring them to the Farr place."

"You're going to Farr's?"

"As fast as a horse can take me," Becky assured her. "Maybe I can get there in time to stop another killing."

"All right, Becky, I can't stop you. I'll get Frank."

Becky ran outside and hurried to the corrals. She threw her saddle on her little black and a spare saddle on one of the work horses. She had just finished when Frank got to the corrals.

"You find Harvey or Clyde or someone, if you have to ride all the way to Santa Fe," she instructed in a firm tone as she handed him the reins of the horse. "If you find Harvey in time to get him to Farr's place, you get him there. At least get Clyde or a deputy out there."

"Becky, I'll do the best I can," Carlson assured her as he stiffly mounted the horse.

"Frank," Becky added in a softer, more natural tone, "be sure to tell Harvey about Clint, who he is and what will happen to him if he gets in a gunfight with Watson. After all he's done for us, we just can't let him ruin his chance at that pardon. I'll try to stall things or do something to keep them apart until Harvey gets there or I can get Clint to come back here."

"Hope you can make it in time, girl."

"Some way, I've got to."

She swung into the saddle as lightly as any cowboy. She rode with Frank a short distance before turning her horse west, while he followed the main road south toward town. She let the little black out to his long trot and stood in the stirrups. She headed straight west, taking the shortest cross-country route to the Farr ranch, never thinking Clint would be heading southwest toward the Payne place.

Sunrise came behind her and spread its light ahead of her. She kept her eyes sweeping from side to side, hoping to get sight of the two riders she was looking for. How desperately she wanted to overtake Clint before he got to Farr's.

It was midmorning when she rode into the Farr ranch. Chickens scattered before the little black horse as she trotted up to the hitch rail in front of the main house. She could see several men working with horses at the corrals. Bud Jarvis was sitting on the bunkhouse porch talking to another rider—she couldn't tell if it was Watson. Clint must not have gotten there yet, for all the activity seemed normal.

Two men came out of the main house and crossed the porch as she swung down and tied the horse. She almost ran through the yard gate and up the walk to meet them as they descended the steps together.

"My, but you're in a big hurry," Carl Farr spoke gently. "What in the world brings you here?"

"I've been expecting you to come see me," Hal Flack said and smiled in good-humored sarcasm. "Somehow, I didn't expect you today."

"Apparently Clint hasn't gotten here yet," Becky said evenly. "I'm glad of that."

"Was he supposed to come here?" queried the Farr foreman, his hawklike eyes suddenly alert and interested.

"Is Watson here?" the girl countered.

"At the bunkhouse. Why?"

"Then, Clint will be here."

"Is your man coming here to try to face Watson?" Farr asked. When she nodded, he continued, "He must be crazy. Are you sure?"

"Yes." Her single answer raised the rancher's eyebrows.

"Well, come on inside where we can talk comfortably, Becky," Farr invited, turning back toward the house. "Mrs. Farr will be glad to see you and we'll have her put on some tea for us."

"No! I have no time for tea!" Becky snapped. "I want you to get Watson out of here, out of the country before Clint gets here. Watson has already killed Monte and that should be enough."

"It surely is, Becky," Farr assured her, turning back toward the woman. "However, it's up to you to control your men. If Monte had not threatened Watson and the others, this would never have happened."

"Monte was shot down in cold-blooded murder, Mr. Farr! I saw it myself." Becky's brown eyes blazed. "I have no time to argue with you! I want to prevent further bloodshed. You've got to get Watson out of the country before Clint gets here."

"If we were to tell Watson to run, your brother would go after him, claiming he was running from fear of arrest,"

Flack cut in. "Your man would be a fool to come in here and face Watson. It would be certain death."

"He left the ranch way before sunup so I wouldn't know what he was doing, but I know he's coming here. Clint thought a lot of Monte, and he knows Payne and Cameron would lie to keep Watson from going to jail."

"Russ and Sid are honest, hard-working ranchers," Farr said with a curt nod of his steel gray head. "They wouldn't lie."

"Let's not argue! I beg you to get rid of that man!"

"What would you give to have us send him away?" Flack asked, a gleam in his eyes. Perhaps now she would realize how important he could be in her life.

"Not what you want, Hal," she replied evenly. "I only want to stop any more killing."

"Well, let's go down to the bunkhouse and see what Watson has to say," Farr suggested. "Maybe he'll leave voluntarily when he hears your man is coming for him."

"Yeah," the foreman added wryly. "He might be scared of Austin."

The three walked to the bunkhouse, a man on each side of Becky. Bud Jarvis left the bunkhouse porch and came to meet them—Watson stayed in his chair against the wall.

"Watson, Miss Major says her man Austin is coming gunnin' for you," Hal Flack said as they neared the bunkhouse porch.

The long-faced rider looked Becky over coldly, his dark eyes going over her from head to toe. He now turned his face slightly, but not his eyes, to spit.

"So?"

"She wants you should get out of the country," the foreman said softly. "She don't want any more killing."

The long-faced rider spat again without taking his eyes off the woman. He spoke to Flack as if Becky weren't there.

"Tell her if her rider leaves me alone, there won't be no more killing."

"We told her that already," Flack said, smiling. "Don't seem to get through to her. She says the only way is for you to get out of the country before her man gets here."

"Well, I ain't runnin' away from any Major hand," Watson scoffed and hooked his bootheels on the rung of the chair. "I've a score to settle with Austin, anyway." As he spoke, the gunman let his finger trace the mark of the rope burn that had split his face. "If he comes here, I'll kill him sure."

"Maybe you will and maybe you won't!" Becky said, loathing the man who killed Monte. "Clint is known as Pecos on the Arrowhead Ranch up in Colorado. From what I understand, he has killed a man or two himself. This time it will be different from the way you shot an old man who had no chance to defend himself!"

"You ever hear of this Arrowhead outfit, Watson?" Flack asked, as he looked sideways at Becky. "You was supposed to be up in Colorado once, wasn't you?"

"Yeah," the gunman's eyes never left Becky's face. "I've heard of that outfit. I've heard of a man called Pecos, too, and he does have a reputation. That whole outfit does. But, I don't believe Austin is the fellow they call Pecos."

"I don't lie like you do!" Becky shouted at him.

"You're some little hellcat in men's clothes, Miss Major!" Watson said as he spoke to her directly for the first time.

"You won't leave, then?" she asked, her eyes blazing hate at him.

"No. I'm not leaving. I'll kill this man just like I did old Monte. Self-defense."

"Well, since you're so all-fired brave, why don't you just shoot me, too?" Becky blazed. "How about adding a woman to the notches on your gun?"

"Oh, now be sensible, Miss Major. Why in the world would anyone take on so over the death of a worthless old man?"

A startled expression suddenly came over the gunman's eyes as, in desperation, Becky reached for her pistol. Even as she made the attempt, she did not know for sure she could pull the trigger. She thought she might at least wound the man, and it was some comfort to think that if he killed her, he would surely have to run for his life, for no court in the West would ever let him off if he killed a woman in a gunfight. Besides, her hatred of the man momentarily overcame her fear of the consequences.

Her gun was just clearing her holster and Watson seemed frozen in disbelief when Flack grabbed her arm. He swung his other arm around her waist and held her tight against him. What a woman, he thought, as he held her trim body against his and forced the gun from her hand.

"Watson, you almost got yourself killed," Flack said, as the unnerved gunman let the chair down and stood up. "This woman's got more pure guts than any man I've ever known. I think, by God, she would have killed you on the spot."

Becky whirled on the foreman then and laid into him with both fists.

"Whoa, there!" the man cried, for the blows hurt. "I just saved you from killing a man!"

He shoved her roughly away from him and she turned to run toward the house.

"You'd better go stop her, Mr. Farr, before she finds another gun," the foreman shouted to his employer. He let his fingers run across his lip, which had been cut by the woman's hard little fists.

"I should have killed her," Watson stormed and stomped across the porch in his frustration and anger.

"If you had, I'd sure have killed you," Flack told him coldly.

"Nobody puts me in a spot like that!" Watson spat out.

"Well, she sure did, Watson. She would have killed you sure, had I not stepped in. Now, you're fired Watson," Flack snapped, his eyes watching the gunman closely. "If this mess means this much to that woman, I'm through fighting her and I think it is time that you get out of here."

"I'm not going anywhere."

"I told you, you are fired."

"I'm not leaving here till I settle with Austin. Besides, Farr hired me and he'll have to be the one to fire me."

"We'll see about that." The tall foreman turned on his heel. He hurried to the hitch rail, where Farr was trying to restrain Becky from untying her horse.

"Wait, Miss Major," Flack urged as he arrived. "I'll go see if I can find Austin for you. I'll try everything I can to persuade him to stay away from here until I can get rid of Watson."

"Are you sure your man was really coming here?" Farr asked again.

"Yes, I'm sure."

"But he didn't actually tell you this?"

"No."

"I have a feeling he just rode off and left the country," Farr now said persuasively. "You'll never hear from him again—I know these drifters."

"Not Clint. Besides, Tim wouldn't leave with him."

"I believe her, Carl. If he really is the man Pecos from the Arrowhead, Watson may be the one who should be scared. Here's your gun, Becky. You stay here in case I miss your man. Maybe you can head off trouble. Any way this turns out, Carl, I'm not fighting the Majors anymore. I've already fired Watson, but he says he won't leave till you tell him, since you're the one who brought him here. I'm through with the whole deal. If you don't like it, you can get yourself another foreman."

"We'll talk about it later, Hal," Farr said sternly.

"That we will," the foreman agreed. "But I'm fed up with this Major deal and I am hereby out of it!"

With this, he turned and went to get his horse. He mounted, put spurs to the animal's sides, and the horse dug in the soft ground in a surprised burst of speed.

Becky and the Farrs spent the balance of the morning on the big porch, where they could watch for any sign of Clint.

From where they sat, they could see Watson still sitting on the tipped-back chair in front of the bunkhouse.

A few hours later two men appeared suddenly, apparently having come up the arroyo beyond the corrals, hidden from those at the bunkhouse and corrals. Becky knew instantly it was Clint and Tim. She ran down the steps to the yard gate, dashing around the post so quickly she almost fell. Then, she watched—the awful scene she had wanted so desperately to stop unfolded before her eyes. Just as in her dream, she could do nothing to stop it. Farr and his wife were running behind her, both shouting for her to stop.

Watson let his chair down and stood up slowly, his scarred face still showing the unnerving experience the woman had given him that morning. He had no real fear, but he was not as confident now as he had been before the episode with the Major woman. Was this man really the Pecos of Arrowhead he had heard about? Perhaps those thoughts slowed his hand ever so slightly as he drew his pistol. The gun cleared his holster smoothly, and he was automatically looking for the spot he intended to send his first shot when the bullet from Austin's gun tore into his chest and he crashed backward, falling heavily over the chair as he crumpled to the porch floor and lay still.

Not a word had been spoken. Inside the bunkhouse, Bud Jarvis jumped to his feet and ran to the doorway. He looked at Clint with what seemed bovine stupidity. He suddenly became aware his Adam's apple was running up and down his throat and he was unable to stop it.

Clint turned his attention to Bud as Tim turned to watch the people running toward the bunkhouse. Bud had never seen such a look as that in Clint's eyes. The only thing Bud could think to do, he did automatically. His hands raised up even with his shoulders.

"I'll not draw!" Bud shouted.

Again, the Colt spoke from Clint's hip, and Jarvis felt a tug and pain at his right hip as the heavy slug tore the holster from his belt to let his gun fall to the door sill where it flipped over outside the door to the ground.

"You once said you wished I'd put on a gun," Clint told the big man coldly. "Well, I have. If I ever catch you on Major land again, I'll use it."

"You'll never find me there again!" Bud whined, wanting to run but having no place to go. "I've had enough!"

Clint turned then as Tim let Becky go to him. The woman rushed up to him and threw her arms around his neck. "Why did you do it?" she cried desperately. "I tried so hard to prevent this. You've ruined your chance of a pardon!"

"It had to be, Becky," he told her softly and let his hand touch her face but forced himself to restrain from his desire to kiss her.

"Riders coming!" Tim warned and Clint turned to look over Becky's head as four horsemen loped toward them, on the road from town.

"It's all right," Clint said recognizing Harvey Major leading the group on his flashy pinto. Frank Carlson's arm flopped with each movement of his horse and the Swede's face wore the pain he had endured on his ride. Clint's face did show some surprise at seeing Hal Flack with them.

Farr stepped forward as the four men drew rein and dismounted.

"Harvey, arrest that man," Farr demanded angrily. "He just shot Watson and maybe Bud!"

"We heard two shots," Harvey admitted evenly.

"I saw it. I saw him shoot them both. You arrest him."

The tall sheriff walked slowly toward his sister and Clint. He turned when he was beside them and looked back at his father-in-law.

"Did Watson admit he shot Monte?" he asked as he put his arm around his sister's shoulder.

"He bragged about it. Besides, I saw him kill Monte in cold blood!" she said, looking up at her brother and was surprised when he looked down and winked at her.

"Hal Flack told us you even tried to shoot Watson yourself," Harvey said, and she would never forget the sparkle in his brown eyes as he smiled down at her.

"I wanted so desperately to keep Clint from losing his chance at a pardon that I lost my head."

"Well, Harvey, are you going to do your duty and arrest that man, or not?" Farr called. "You're the sheriff, so start acting like it."

Clint was suddenly aware Harvey's hand had grasped his wrist and slid down to put something into his hand. Clint's fingers tightened on a metal object.

"Why, I've got no call to arrest my own deputy," the tall sheriff stated slowly. "Show Carl your badge, Clint."

Clint looked down as he turned his hand palm up. The sunlight glinted on the silver shield and his eyes read the word "Sheriff" across the badge. Clint flashed the badge toward the rancher, then lifted his hand to stick the badge in his shirt pocket.

"Clint's been working for me for some time," Harvey said easily. "I'm proud of him, too. He's done a good job. I am sure he would have arrested Watson if the man hadn't tried to shoot him."

"Who in the world would ever believe that?" Farr demanded, his eyes going over his son-in-law's face.

"Well, I would for one," Tim Harding spoke up. "Remember, Carl, I was here, too—closer to what happened than you were. Clint had to shoot or be killed, himself. Watson gave him no choice."

"I believe that," Hal Flack stated firmly, his eyes meeting his employer's squarely.

"I don't like it, Harvey," Farr began.

"Then stay out of it," Harvey cut in bluntly. "I'm not near as concerned about that deal in Santa Fe as you may think. I'm pretty happy just being sheriff. You've got no claim on me. Beth knows how I feel and she'll be happy here if she has to. I'll do my job as I see fit. My deputy attempted an arrest and was forced to kill the man in self-defense. Besides, if I understand this, you were behind it all, anyway. Kind of makes me the fool for having forced the family to take your money. Now perhaps you had best remember what family your daughter married into. We Majors stick together on things and I sure don't like the idea of my father-in-law trying to steal Major range."

Hal Flack walked forward and stopped a short distance in front of Becky.

"I'm sorry I didn't find Austin in time for you, Becky," he said very politely. "At least, I tried. I've already told you and Carl I'm through with this deal. No more trying to force you off your range, as far as I'm concerned. I'll see Smokey Bennett understands, too."

"We've already delivered a message to him," Clint said slowly. "Thanks, anyway. Without you, I don't think the Farr outfit amounts to much."

"You're a lucky man, Austin." Flack turned to Clint. "Any woman who would take the chance to save you as Becky did today is pure gold. I've never known one like her."

Hal Flack stuck out his hand and Clint accepted it with a firm grip.

"Well, let's get out of here and get back to where we belong," Harvey said. "I'll send the undertaker out for Watson."

Becky stayed in town for a few days after Monte's funeral. Clint returned to the ranch, along with Juan who was now strong enough to return to work. Frank and Helen Carlson moved back into their home in town, where Helen would keep Little Harvey and Susan until school started. There was a letter from Vance saying he was coming home soon since his leg was now healing nicely, and he would be able to take over the ranch again when he returned.

Tim Harding came by Becky's house in town to say good-bye. He was returning to his own home. Their farewell was sad for Tim, because he knew he had lost her, but he was still proud he had come to her aid.

Becky returned to the ranch in midafternoon of another beautiful Indian summer day. The ranch house was deserted, and she went to her room to change into the men's clothing that had become so much a part of her life for the past few months. She returned to the buggy and carried the many supplies she had brought into the kitchen and put them away, then put the buggy under the shed and unharnessed the team and turned them out to pasture.

Back in the kitchen Becky built a fire in the big range and soon the aroma of baking filled the air. It had been some time since she had baked a cake but she had not lost her touch. When the men rode in as the sun was dropping in the west, their meal was ready. Afterward, Clint and Juan insisted on doing the dishes and Becky went outside to enjoy the twilight and sunset. She walked around the corner to the outside door of her room and sat down on the step, bringing her knees up under her chin and wrapping her arms around her legs.

She listened for the sound of the nighthawks, and sure enough she heard one booming in the distance. The mournful call of doves came to her ears and from somewhere near the corrals came the soft hoot of an owl. In the distance coyotes howled their feeling into the evening air. Looking toward the sunset, she saw a whirlwind lifting its dust high into the air as it moved slowly across the rim of the basin. The sun's rays caught the dust particles and turned them into crimson sparkles of light, and she drank in the sight, enjoying every moment. Winter would soon be here and she would think back to this night.

The sound of Clint's spurs came to her moments before he turned the corner of the house.

"It's a beautiful evening, Clint," she said, her chin on her folded arms.

"Yes, ma'am."

He came closer but stood above her, not attempting to sit beside her.

" 'Yes ma'am'?" she said. "Don't tell me we're back to that."

"Oh, I know my place now," he said, making sure she would know he was teasing. "Your dad never let you have anything to do with the hired help."

She winced at this even though she recognized his teasing. She saw him hold something out to her. It shown brightly in the dim light.

"Give this back to your brother," he said slowly. "I really appreciate what Harvey did. I hope I can convince the governor I was a deputy when I used my gun, even though it is not completely true."

"Harvey said for you to keep the badge as a memento, show it to the governor, maybe. He also sent out a letter stating he had hired you as a special deputy over a month ago, just in case you need it. You know, he told me he had intended to offer you a badge the next time he saw you, anyhow."

"That's mighty nice of him."

"Well, he knows the risk you took, Clint. We all owe you much more than we will ever be able to repay," she said and motioned for him to sit beside her. It was dark enough now, that he could barely make out the outline of her face against the sky. "Well, what will you do after you get things squared away in Colorado? Will you come back here?"

He thought for a moment, trying to find the right words. "I doubt I'll come back here," he said at length. "Your brother will be home shortly. There will be no place for me here. Besides, Arrowhead is my home, my friends are there."

"This ranch is partly mine—I'm sure we can pay you foreman's wages. I wish it could be more."

"I'd still be a hired hand to your brother, Becky. Your father's rule really wasn't a bad one."

"I've already told you, you were the exception to prove the rule."

"I know, but there would still be a chance the rest of the family would resent me here on the ranch. Even Vance can't stop the changing of time. The open range is soon going to be a thing of the past. Your family will have to homestead or some way get actual title to much more land. If you don't, the others will eventually push in on you, no matter how tough you are. Owning the land will cost more in taxes and fencing. It means you can develop better cattle but it also means smaller spreads. There will be no place here for me for long. But, at least you can say we saved it for your family to run as long as they can."

"And at Arrowhead there will be a place for you?"

"Yes, I do think so. I was assistant foreman when I left. I might get that job back someday. Maybe the foreman's job or even manager. It's all private land already, you see—it was originally a Spanish land grant. Taxes cost a lot but you can fence it and do what you want with it. Clay Hamilton is a darn good rancher—a smart one too—and I do see a future there. He is already improving the cattle, using top-notch bulls. He don't have to worry about what bulls his neighbors use and he is a good man to work for."

"So, you'll just stay in Colorado?" Her tone was matter of fact, as though she had accepted it.

"I expect so."

"When do you plan to leave?"

"As soon as Vance gets here."

They were silent for a moment.

"I wish so much things were different, Becky," he said softly, and sat down beside her. "I wish I had something worthwhile to offer a woman. You'll never know how proud I was about your standing up to Watson."

"I guess it has all worked out for the best, but I wanted so desperately to keep you from ruining your chance at that pardon . . . or being killed."

"I know."

"I'm glad it's over. I don't like killing but Watson got what he deserved and I'm only glad you were not hurt."

Again silence descended over them. Both wanted to say more and each tried to find the words they wanted. Finally, they both started to speak at the same time and had to laugh at the awkwardness of the moment.

"Becky, I've got to know," he said after another pause. "Will you marry me, that is if I get the pardon, of course? I've loved you since about the first time I ever saw you. Arrowhead has some housing for married men. Nothing fancy but . . ."

"You know how fancy I am. How could you love a woman who looks, rides, and lives like a cowhand?"

"You look mighty pretty in a dress but I've learned to love you for what you are. You're more woman than anyone I've ever known. I'll go to Colorado and take care of things up there. Then, if I get pardoned, I'll send for you, if you'll have me."

"Not on your life, you won't!"

"What?"

"Do you think for one minute I'll wait around here while you're up there chasing some old girlfriend you never told me about? Not on your life, cowboy! If I'm going, I'm going with you when you go and I'm going as your wife! The governor can pardon you just as well married as single."

"Gentlemen hush!" he exclaimed. "What happens if the governor don't pardon me?"

"Well, if that happens, we'll just have to ride on somewhere else—you can't ride anyplace I can't."

"I'll sure not argue with that. Maybe with you coaching me I can get the foreman's job, after all," he said as she snuggled against him.

"Why not go for the manager's?" she asked. "You might just as well go for broke, cowboy."

"I think I already have."